Small Circle of Beings

Damon Galgut was born in Pretoria in 1963. He wrote his first novel, *A Sinless Season*, when he was seventeen. His other books include *Small Circle of Beings*, *The Beautiful Screaming of Pigs*, *The Quarry*, *The Good Doctor*, *The Impostor*, *In A Strange Room* and *Arctic Summer*. *The Good Doctor* was shortlisted for the Man Booker Prize and the Dublin/IMPAC Award and won the Commonwealth Writers' Prize (Africa region), *The Impostor* was shortlisted for the Commonwealth Writers' Prize (Africa region) and *In a Strange Room* was shortlisted for the Man Booker Prize. He lives in Cape Town.

ALSO BY DAMON GALGUT

A Sinless Season

The Beautiful Screaming of Pigs

The Quarry

The Good Doctor

The Impostor

In a Strange Room

Arctic Summer

DAMON GALGUT
Small Circle of Beings

Atlantic Books
London

First published by Contable & Company Ltd, Great Britain 1988.
Published in Abacus by Sphere Books Ltd 1990.
Revised edition published by Penguin Books (South Africa) (Pty) Ltd 2005.

This paperback edition published by Atlantic Books in 2015

1 3 5 7 9 8 6 4 2

A CIP catalogue record for this book is available
from the British Library.

Paperback ISBN: 978 1 78239 631 4
E-book ISBN: 978 0 85789 175 4

Printed and bound in Barcelona by Novoprint S.A.

Atlantic Books
An imprint of Atlantic Books Ltd
Ormond House
26-27 Boswell Street
London
WC1N 3JZ

www.atlantic-books.co.uk

CONTENTS

Small Circle of Beings

Is love so small a pain, do you think, for a woman?

Medea – by Euripides

To my mother

ONE

1

He falls ill on a day like any other. He comes to me where I sit in the high arched window, looking down the valley. He points to his stomach, lifting up his shirt.

'I have a pain,' he says.

I look at his smooth white skin. I bend my head and kiss him there, next to the wrinkled hole of his belly button. He smells of sand.

'There,' I say. 'It'll go away now.'

But it doesn't. It's the very next day that he comes back to me – I forget where I am sitting, perhaps in the same place at the window, or at the kitchen table, peeling onions – and says:

'It's still there.'

He's such a little boy. At times when I look at him while he's busy with other things, I can see in his face the clues of inheritance: my father's frown, my mother's smile. Stephen's mouth. But I cannot, for some reason, catch a glimpse of myself in him, in his narrow dark head, his round pale eyes a little too far apart.

'David,' I say. 'It'll go away.'

'It doesn't,' he says. 'I wait, but it doesn't go.'

'Do you want some medicine?'

'Yes,' he says. 'Medicine.'

I give him a Disprin to take away the pain. And for a few hours it seems to help. I can see him from the window where I sit, as he plays alone on the lawn outside. There's a strong wind blowing and leaves go skimming across the grass.

This is where we live. There is David and myself, and there is Stephen, who is my husband. We have lived here for ten years now, in this stone-walled house with its roof of thatch. (It is the stones I love most, round and grey as bubbles.) The house is far out of town, at the end of the dust road that goes up into the mountains. There are other houses farther down the valley, but the nearest is two kilometres away. From the window where I like to sit there's a view only of slopes covered in forest. On clear days you can see the dam in the distance, silver and still. But usually the days aren't clear; the air is thick with heat or mist. In summer it rains.

We grow fruit and vegetables in the cleared acre below the house. I like to stand there with the round shapes of avocados swelling in the air above my head. There are carrots too, and lettuce. Farther down the hill are tomatoes, beetroot, onion. There are grapefruit trees. The planted rows, hacked out of the earth, go winding round the hill. I stand and survey them from the top of the slope. Scents rise to my nose, leaking out of fissures in the ground. Berries. Petals.

It's a wild land, this. At the edges of the tamed space a dense wall of jungle rises, woven with leaves so that it seems impenetrable. But this is not the case: there are paths that lead into the forest, if you know where to look. I've walked most of them by now. Often, without conscious reason, I find myself on a narrow track leading off under the trees and am compelled to follow. Below the house, a few hours' walk, is a lake much smaller than the dam I can see from the window. Above the house the forest continues in successive tiers, building in dark layers toward the stony crests of the hills. I haven't been far that way; there is something truly primitive in the vegetation here. The earth too is black and secret, boiling with roots like the surface of a deep, infested sea.

It's from up here, from its occult sources in the tops of the mountains, that the bad weather comes. It rolls down towards us in a thick white cloud, absolutely silent, tumbling in perfect slow motion across the carpet of trees. In half an hour the mist is sliding all about the house. Stranded and afloat, we are freed from our moorings on the ground for a little time.

If you wander off to the right of the house, the forest is fairly thin. There are pine trees here, so no undergrowth grows to catch the feet. But the needles also lie in deep brown drifts, covering over the path like snow. It is possible to walk for a long way in the gloomy green light, under a dark roof upheld by the trunks of trees. If you go far enough, however, the trees do come to an end, and you will find yourself at the edge of a scrubby field that leads down to plantations of trees far larger than ours. Our territory ends here and the neighbouring farm begins. It's a pleasant place to stand, giving a view of cultivated lands arranged in patterns discernible only from here, so high. Labourers work there among the trees, picking the fruit as if to feed an endless hunger. But it isn't theirs.

To the left of the house, the path goes only a little way. Then you come to a cluster of huts, daubed with paint and thatched with grass. A community lives there, but one I do not understand. There are men, women and a great many children. There are chickens and goats. A continual clamour rises from this place: a noise of shouting, singing, clucking and banging. On certain nights there is a radio playing, but the music is harsh and strange. I can hear it from the house, from the open window where I like to sit. There have been nights when the sound of this music has pierced me like a chill, so that I have to rub myself to stay warm. I've been only seldom to the huts, though they are closer to me in distance than any of the real neighbours I have. I don't like it there and the people look at me strangely. They are as odd as their dwellings, with their flat bony faces and shiny black skin. They speak a different language. They do not like me.

When *they* are ill, they consult a doctor who lives alone in the jungle above the house. Or so I am told. I think of this man, this hermit, who inhabits, I imagine, a cave of some sort, a recess in the rock. Although I have never seen him, I dare to picture him in my head: tall and thin, hung about with beads and skins. His nails are long. When he looks at me (which he does in dreams, I must confess), his eyes are luminous and large. Too large. They look into me and see all that I would try to hide from such a gaze as this: my willingness, above all, to believe in his magic.

There is something in me that finds all this attractive. Yes. From the first, before David falls ill, I respond to the power of herbs, of fire, of spells cast in the dark. There is that in me which sees a logic in the tossing of bones, the patterns of entrails on the ground. But I know, too, that this is shameful and absurd. No white woman, no matter how far out of town she may live, can have respect for the rituals of these inscrutable dark people. It is better by far to be afraid of them.

So I avoid the cluster of huts. My only contact with them for over a year now has been in the fact that my servants live there. But they are only two out of a great many. Each morning, promptly at eight, half an hour after Stephen has disappeared down the road in his car, they appear from the leaves at the edge of the grass that surrounds the house. They walk one behind the other, not talking or touching.

That is their way. Salome and Moses. Nothing like their biblical fellows, this pair is old and dour. They wear torn clothes with no regard for colour or appearance. They put on overalls to protect themselves from dirt as they work. I give them their tasks. Salome's domain is inside, within the walls. I set her to polishing, to sweeping, to scrubbing. Usually I supervise her in her labour, but there are days when I join her. In a rush of energy I roll up my sleeves and fall to my knees. Alongside her, so close that our flanks are touching, I help to scrub the floor. It's at times like these, in the friction of bristles on the boards, or the sudden accidental collision of our hips, that I feel closest to her. She has, on such an occasion, smiled at me.

For the most part, though, she seems not to like me much. She is polite enough, dipping her head and cupping her hands in thanks when I give her a gift. This happens at Christmas or at Easter, the holidays we like to observe. There are other times, though, when I will give her a present out of sheer impulsive charity. Out of, I sometimes suspect, a need to exact something more from her than this reserved deference, this dipping of her head. I give her old clothes. I give her money. Once, in a fit of absurd generosity, I pressed into her hands a book. She looked at me then: a glance of direct surprise. But she did not yield up her gratitude. She merely, as usual, bent her head and accepted the token with those same cupped hands, muttering acknowledgement as if I had presented her with something utterly worthless.

Which perhaps I had.

Moses is, if anything, less pleasant than she. He is a short fat man, whose tight curly hair is turning grey on top. He hardly ever speaks, responding to the orders I give him with a small, compressed blinking of his eyes. He never looks directly at me, but turns his gaze out sideways, focusing on something beyond my sight, behind and to the left of me. I don't like Moses. There is something menacing in his quietness. Or perhaps it is in the size of his hands, which are as large as steaks. His nails are broad. I watch him sometimes from my seat in the high arched window as he tends to the garden. For this is his place of work: the cultivated moat of green around the house that separates us from the encroaching jungle beyond. There are flowerbeds here. I have planted daisies, lilies, carpets of poppies. At the verge of the bottom lawn there is a wide deep bed. Roses are planted here. They give off a scent: a raw but elegant smell that drifts on the air like invisible colour.

Moses tends the garden. He does so without love, without the slightest indication of interest. I've watched him from my window as he moves between the flowerbeds, trailing in one hand the brutal blades of the shears. His feet are heavy as he walks. Yet there is in his rough hands a kind of tenderness I cannot see. The garden grows. At his hard touch, the flowers burst open like blobs of paint. The leaves jostle and surge. It makes me unhappy to see; I who would do the same, but who cannot understand his secrets. I am gentle with the plants, I mind them carefully. But, under my care, they wilt and die. There is nothing I can do. It is for me to plan the garden, to envisage the arrangements of colour and the shapes of the beds. It is for Moses, squat, untalkative Moses, to watch the seeds.

For all of this, I would be happy to let him go. I am, I think, afraid of him. I believe him capable of things, of deeds I try not to imagine. Though he is married, I believe, to the harmless Salome. (What do they talk about as they lie in bed, I wonder? Is it me? Do their tongues at last break loose and say mocking, malicious things about me, their ridiculous figure of a mistress, that keep them giggling long into the night?)

But there is another reason, apart from the flowers, that I cannot dispense with this man.

There is, you see, one other person in this place, who inhabits the area with us. It is difficult for me sometimes to regard her as entirely human, despite the evidence of her four limbs and her face. This person is my mother. When I was a little girl, all of thirty years ago, although she stood over me, pale and bloodless as a figure carved from ice, I barely noticed her. Now she is always at the edges of my sight, sidling along the verges of flowerbeds, creeping next to the walls. It is all I can do to ignore her. By some bizarre trick of fate, now that she is truly at the very perimeter of my life, she looms larger in my mind than she ever did before.

My mother is mad. This condition beset her one day, one evening, as she went about her existence with the calm of habit. Or so it seemed to me. Actually – as I was told afterward by the doctor who treated her – her madness advanced on her by the slowest degrees. It took over her mind, the doctor said, bit by bit, but became evident to those around her only when it passed a certain point. That point was reached one evening, when at the supper table she picked up her plate and hurled it with startling force against the far wall. It was still full of food, which sprayed out in intricate patterns across the floor. There were guests present, one of whom was myself (I had left home already and was living alone in town), and we sat in amazed silence and stared at her where she stood, napkin in hand. Oh, she was a beautiful woman, my mother, even then: a serene figure, with a wooden face that belonged on the prow of a ship. She smiled.

'It was poisoned,' she said.

She has lost that beauty since then. For a time she continued to live alone in this too-huge house, managing affairs with reasonable competence. But it became increasingly clear that events had fallen beyond her grasp. When she'd spoken of poison, she was referring not to her food, but to her daily existence in this lonely house on the hill.

People were out to get her, she told me (on my regular visits from my little flat in town). Old friends desired her wealth. Murderers lurked beneath the bed. She wept at night. I knew my duty and I faced it with bitter calm. There was nothing I wanted more than for her to die and vanish. Nevertheless, I packed up my belongings and, in a single day, moved back here, to the home in which I'd grown up and which I'd left for ever just two short years before. I looked after her. I cared for her as completely as I had any of the flowers in the garden outside, and she wilted as quickly at my touch. The madness progressed. I observed its daily triumph as the things on which she'd once prided herself began to go bad. Her frosty, backswept hair went unbrushed and unwashed. Her long, thin nails, painted grey, were bitten to the quick. Her jewellery and dresses, boxes and cupboards of them, were untouched; she wore a single slacksuit, blue at first, but growing darker and darker as it was left dirty. Her body, too, decayed: that skin, with its lustre, its high silver sheen, became cracked and loose, as if it were the covering of some larger mysterious creature beneath that was trying to break out. She smells, I hate to say; when she comes near to me, I have to breathe through my mouth. And, wherever she goes, she is followed by a decrepit, tattered poodle, blind in one eye and lame in two legs, that totters behind her like a diminutive parody. This dog was once a pampered, powdered beast, tied up with ribbons; it was the object of her most absurd affection. It cannot understand its own demise any more than hers, but limps around in the hope, I suppose, that its day will return.

(There is an irony that does not escape me: all that most angered me about my mother when I was young has decayed now, and is the source of my greatest shame.)

All this simply to explain: Moses is a servant as old as this house. He worked here when my mother was a child and being raised by *her* mother. There is – how, I do not know, but there is – a pact between Moses and the mad old woman that will defy my wants. I cannot get rid of him. It would break my mother's heart. On the days that he doesn't come in, Sundays or other holidays, she is almost beside herself. She wanders about the lawn, calling to him in a voice as strained and thin as the cry of a bird.

So I endure this man. From the time that he arrives in the morning I have little trouble from my mother, who stays close to him in order to keep an eye. Even when she doesn't follow him around, she hangs about the window of her back room and peers out at him through the curtains. She lives back here, in a separate flatlet once used to house guests. She moved there when I married Stephen, shortly after I returned home. She hates my husband. I think she always did, even before her madness took command. Why I cannot say; he's always been good to her. But he evokes in her an irrational response that leads her to make up extraordinary tales. Often she has taken me aside with an air of grim frenzy, and warned me that Stephen is plotting to kill me. She has seen him, she says, mixing poisons in the kitchen while I'm out. A few times she has seen him paying Salome to stab me.

All of this I hear with amusement, and fear. Her thoughts are insane, but they are based on fact: Stephen mixes drinks in the kitchen, he gives Salome her wages. This is the form of my mother's madness: it distorts the meaning of what she sees.

But I pity her her mind. What terrible visions she must have when the wind moves the leaves outside her window at night. Certain sights appal her. She cannot bear it, for instance, when Moses mows the lawn. For some inexplicable reason, probably least known to herself, Moses pushing the mower causes her great distress. For this I have found a bizarre solution: for the past three years now this chore has been done under cover of darkness. Every few weeks, on a night with a clear moon, Moses mows the lawn. It is, you may well believe, a strange and wonderful sight: the squat black man gliding across the moonlit lawn. While my mother, unsuspecting, sits in her room and dreams.

I did not wish to raise the subject of my mother now, and have discussed her in far greater depth than I intended, but there is another thing that must be said, if only in passing. I have been told by the doctor who treated her that her madness is not entirely explicable. He suspects, however, that it is a hereditary thing. I think at once of my mother's sister, my aunt, whom I did not know well, but who is, I believe, in an institution somewhere. And so confirm this doctor's veiled warning, if only in my own mind: I too shall be mad. There will come a time in my life when, unbeknown to myself, my comprehension of events will begin to change in subtle ways. I will fail to grasp the true significance of words. People will threaten me, will plan my downfall behind my back. The thought of this is terrible to me: I cry. Stephen tries to comfort me, but there is nothing he can really say. If this will happen, it will happen despite my will.

I have by now, of course, accepted the idea. At times it seems an interesting notion: to endure the shrinking of my brain until my world is an acre of lawn and two dirty rooms. Who will care for me then? Stephen, perhaps? Or David? It's possible even that Moses will relent and take me under his wing. Perhaps I will reach a reconciliation with my mother, and we will sit and drink tea together, cackling to ourselves, while the lawn is being mowed outside. At other times the idea repulses me: I think of myself as she is now, and feel ill. I want to wash, I want to change my clothes. I want to be seen as a person with pride.

To protect myself from this eventuality, I guard my thoughts. I constantly test what I believe, asking myself: can this be true?' Is this so? In such a manner do I hope to put off what may be inevitable. But, for now, I am safe.

So there are, in fact, the six of us: Stephen, David, my mother and I. Salome and Moses. Between us we see to the running of the house. We maintain relations. We keep things safe.

This is the way it is.

By the time Stephen gets home in the late afternoon, I have put David to bed. He's been complaining that the pain has returned. The Disprin that I gave him has failed to work. He doesn't feel hot to me, but there is no reason to disbelieve him. I sit by him in the bed and read to him. Later he falls asleep. When I hear the noise of the bakkie outside, I get up and go out.

Stephen stands on the back lawn outside the garage.

'David is ill,' I tell him.

'What's the matter?'

'Nothing,' I say. 'I don't think it's serious. Don't look now, but my mother is watching.'

He does look. She is crouched at her window, staring out from beneath a lifted corner of the curtain. As our eyes meet hers, the curtain falls.

I put my arm about him. Together we go inside.

2

A cry in the night. Perhaps I have been waiting for it: I am instantly awake and fumbling for my gown. I wrap myself in it, and stumble barefooted across the wooden boards to David's room. He's sitting up in bed, the sheets thrown aside.

The pain, he says, is still there.

I sit by him and murmur to him till he falls asleep. This takes a long time; he whimpers to himself, he bleats. I stroke his head with a rhythmical hand, back and forth. Eventually he subsides into the pillows. His head falls aside, distilling his dreams.

In the morning he seems to be all right. The pain is gone. I help him dress for school (though he's old enough to do this for himself). As he and Stephen drive off I stand at the window and watch them go. David looks up and I shrink back where he cannot see me.

When I fetch David from school after lunch, he's waiting for me on the curb, his chin on his knees. I haven't been thinking about it, but as we drive back up the long dust road, I say to him: 'How is the pain?'

'Gone,' he says. He seems preoccupied and I don't question him further.

It's later, after he's eaten, that he says, looking at me over the table: 'Red came out.'

'What?' I say.

He tells me. In the cloakroom at break, as he stood at the urinal, a stream of red came from his body. What frightened him more was the reaction of the other boys. The row of them along the trough, as they saw the bright flow pass by their feet, turned their heads one by one to look at David. He recalls with vague alarm the faces turned toward him, staring with open mouths.

'They *watched*,' he says.

I feel a rush of pity for him, this little boy who contrived by means beyond his control to piss blood.

'Did it hurt?' I say.

'It burned,' he says. 'A little bit.'

Something is wrong. I take David that same afternoon to see the doctor. Because I don't know another, we consult the same doctor who treated my mother. It's been a long time since I saw him last, but he hasn't changed much.

He's a little man whose body is made up of circles. He has round cheeks, a bald head, and two perfectly round eyes behind round spectacles. His name is Doctor Bouch. He makes David undress and lie on the table. Then he proceeds to examine him, going over the surface of his body with the soft tips of his fingers and the cold steel ends of his instruments. As I stand by, watching, clutching my handbag to my stomach, I catch David's eye and smile. He doesn't smile back.

When he has finished, Dr Bouch tells me that he can find nothing wrong. 'It happens,' he says, 'from time to time.' People pass blood in their water. The pain, he says, 'could be anything'. But it's likely to be minor. I am to call again if it comes back. Before we go, Dr Bouch smiles broadly and asks after my mother.

There is nothing to be done. Life goes on. I accept with relief Dr Bouch's pronouncement on the health of my son, and we return home. In the day to day living on the farm, there is much to be seen to. From the time that David and Stephen leave in the mornings, I am busy with tasks in and about the house. I don't know that Stephen can understand the countless little labours that go into maintaining our existence in this place. Every day, with the help of Salome, there is washing and dusting to be done. Armed with cloths, brushes, mops and water, we apply ourselves to the surfaces about us. We scour them clean of the dirt that, grain by grain, invades us from outside. I have a large collection of silverware that I clean each day. I wipe and polish trays and beakers until my face shines back at me. I smile at my reflection.

It's not a remarkable face. When I was younger I used to wish for features that were interesting, if not beautiful. But there is something bland in my appearance, as though I have not lived deeply enough. My mouth is straight. My eyes are brown. My hair is also brown, brushed back straight from my forehead and tucked behind my ears. I don't like to wear makeup; it hardly seems necessary up here, so far from anyone else. When I have to go into town to do shopping or pay bills, I usually do put a little colour into my face. I touch up my lips, redden my cheeks.

These occasions please Stephen. On the evenings of these days he looks at me and says, 'There now. Why can't you look like that every day?'

'For you?' I say.

'Yes,' he says. 'For me. When I first met you, you used to wear makeup every day.'

This is true. There was a time in my life when I took pride in things like this: I covered my face in powders and oils. I dabbed scent on my wrists and on the back of my neck. I wore long dresses and high-heeled shoes. I was conscious, you could say, of the way I appeared.

But here, in my house in the hills, I seem somehow to have lost myself. I wear flat shoes. I wear old dresses and aprons. In my battle with the dust, I put on the armour of housewives. There are times when I am frightened of myself. I take off my clothes and stand before the mirror. I scrutinise my body, examining my sagging flesh. Gravity has had its effect. As I grow farther and farther from my birth, my body succumbs to the pull of the earth. It melts from my bones and begins to drip and ooze downward under my clothes.

Can this be pleasant for Stephen, I wonder? Does he look at me sometimes and see, as I do, the dowdy little woman I have become? Am I unpleasant for him?

When I worry in this way, I make an effort for him. There are nights, yes, when I dress up in pretty clothes, when I paint my face the way he wants me to do. I put on stockings. I pin up my hair and am, if only for a few hours, the girl he met ten years ago. I am once again Miss Roper, the laughing schoolteacher who somehow seduced him. But there is something false about these evenings, no matter how much he claims to like them. It is as if I am only dressing up, as if I'm putting on a costume in which I no longer belong.

There is, you see, something about the place in which we live that makes pretension impossible. Stephen spends his day in town, in the little office at school where he is headmaster. He cannot know, as I do, the rigours of a life removed. I am far from town. I see few people, other than those I have described. I live, as it were, with necessities. There is no need for makeup or special clothes. There is no one to impress.

Stephen, I suspect, would like to live in town where things are orderly and neat. He would like to attend bridge evenings, go to dinner parties with friends. He has spoken from time to time about moving back there. 'One of the outlying suburbs,' he says. But I can't do it. This house belongs to the family, I tell him. My mother has lived here all her life, as hers did. We can't give it up. Besides, I say, what would Mother do in town? Here she can wander all she likes without getting into trouble. It's safer by far to live here.

In reality, I love this place, with its wild views down the valley, the storms that come down from the hills. I have discovered something of myself in the solitude. Here I am not answerable to people or to custom. I can do as I please. I am my own woman.

I must concede, then, that perhaps a division existed in our marriage long before the sickness began. Perhaps, in our battle of wills, our daily unspoken compromises, there was a fault for which I had to pay, whether or not David fell ill.

But he does fall ill. It becomes clear that something larger and more frightening than I first supposed has entered into his body, and our lives. The pain, the little pain which was the first warning of our downfall, has not gone away. Instead it grows, day by day. The morning after Dr Bouch has made his proclamation, the ache is back. David cries. And it's then, as I gaze at him where he stands in the centre of his room, holding in one hand his grey school shirt and in the other the place in his stomach that is sore, that a revelation comes to me: something has begun. There are secret, subtle nerves between us through which messages and signals are transmitted. As I stand in his bedroom, looking helplessly down at him, I experience a flash of hurt in my body that corresponds in some way with that in his. I go down on one knee and hug him. His arms go round me and he cries.

Chains do exist. People are bound. Nine years ago I gave

birth to this boy. Over the months – eight and a half of them – the weeks, the days, that I carried him, he became part of me in elemental cellular ways. I gave him up when the time was due, expelling him from the cave with strong round rings of muscle. But his presence remains. Sometimes at night, lying awake, I can will myself to recall the sensation of his weight, and I feel the kick of a foot, the shift of a limb, beneath my skin. He continues to live in me, not yet discharged. I am his haven and his prison. He will never leave alive, despite the evidence of this child, nine years of age, who is crying now in my arms. I rock him gently, murmuring in his ear. His nose is running and it gums wetly against my neck.

'Shh now,' I say. 'I'll make it all better.'

But he goes on crying. Till then, a word from me would have been enough to comfort him. Now he's learnt, perhaps, that I lie.

He doesn't go to school that day. I take him instead back to Dr Bouch's rooms, where the little man lays him out on the table and examines him again. He's not as light-hearted this time about his task. He sees in me, I think, a determination he hasn't bargained for. He takes a urine sample. And blood: we watch, David and I, as the pale syringe sucks fluid from his arm.

The results of the tests will be phoned through. But, other than that, Dr Bouch can 'still find nothing wrong'. He looks at me over the top of his desk, contemplative. There is that in his glance which suggests he is sorry, truly sorry, he can find no sickness in my son.

I take David home. I put him to bed. For the first few days he is calm. The pain seems to come to him at particular moments, or times of the day: late afternoons, mostly, and late at night. Then he cries. But otherwise a placid ritual evolves that has as its centre the child in the bed. I go in and out of the room on numerous little missions, bearing trays of tea, plates of snacks. I sit with him. I read to him often from books I buy in town. He's always enjoyed reading; the sound of words excites him. At other times we talk, but on subjects that he chooses. In the morning and at noon, Salome takes proper meals to him, also on a tray. She clears them later. My mother, on her wanderings about the house, discovers his constant presence in the tiny room at the end of the passage. She too takes to visiting, and I often come in to find her sitting in my chair next to the bed. 'Come in,' she says. 'Sammy and I were talking about weddings.'

'My name is David,' he says, and giggles.

Sammy is the name of my father, who died when I was ten years old. There is a photograph of him on the wall above the fireplace, amongst the many others of our family gone past. When I look at this particular photograph I see a man with swollen dark eyes and balding head. His mouth was cruel, but his smile seemed kind enough. I remember little of him, too little. I need to know more, but there is nowhere to find out. Only from my mother who sometimes, in her convoluted ramblings, lets slip a truthful word.

'This is David,' she says now, and grins at me with her turtle's mouth.

I don't like to sit with David and my mother. There is between them, I'm afraid to say, a coded communication which I'm not party to. They get on well. They speak of things I do not understand. 'The roses,' my mother says, 'are full of worms.' She prods at David under the blankets with a long jointless finger, and they laugh merrily together, showing their teeth.

I don't laugh. I'm jealous of them, I have to concede, though why I couldn't say. I suppose I resent the fact that

David is so easy with her, that they like each other so much. My mother was never this good to me as a child, not when she was sane.

I talk to David about it. 'Does she bother you,' I ask, 'with all her mad stories?'

'She isn't mad,' he says. 'She's clever.'

He holds my arm as he says this and speaks so completely earnestly that I become angry.

'Of course she's mad,' I cry. 'She's as mad as a hatter.'

At this he begins to snivel. After a moment I pat his head. I'm ashamed of myself and the ancient anger I'm venting on him. He doesn't know better and if she's a good companion to him, why should I complain? So, after this occasion, I try not to mind so much when I find her drowsing in that chair like a woman long dead.

Stephen, however, will not go in while she's there. She always leaves a room when he enters it, casting backward glances and muttering. He finds her reaction uncomfortable, being an upright man with a sense of order. He stands by this.

'Decency,' he once told me, 'is a sense of order.'

With decency, then, Stephen runs his life. He is concerned for David, but not as concerned as I. He does not believe in fate or things inescapable. Life, he would maintain, is a mathematical affair. Emotions are algebra. There are sums by which one lives and by which, eventually, one dies. There is a logic to this comprehension: he was, after all, a maths teacher for most of his working life, until he became headmaster of the high-school in town. He was a maths teacher when I met him, ten years ago: a thin, tall man with short black hair and a huge black moustache through which he breathed. His eyes, then as now, were lidless and huge. They saw everything there was to see.

He does not get on with David. He loves him, I hasten to say – but this is perhaps the problem. Stephen doesn't know what to do with his love. He whittles it down to dry and brittle words. He refrains from touching David, but keeps his distance and speaks of silly things. David senses this. He finds it difficult to respond, to demonstrate his need for a father he can hug, or talk to, or build kites with. So between them is a rigid trade of thoughts, but never touch.

(Which leads *me* to a thought: Stephen, who has become so comfortable with me, who talks with me and touches me with ease, does he love me still? I have no way of knowing.)

Now, when he comes home from school in the late afternoon, Stephen goes into David's room. He stands awkwardly next to the bed, pulling at his hands as if to rid them of their skin.

'How do you feel today?' he asks. 'Are you better than yesterday?'

Or:

'I had a terrible time today. So many bad boys in the office. You're not going to be a bad boy, are you, when you grow up?'

To which David smiles and says no.

Stephen doesn't stay in there long. He comes out after fifteen minutes or so and goes to change. He takes off the tight blue suits he wears daily to school and which give him an implacable air, like a man in command. He dresses in casual clothes: shorts and sandals, T-shirts or vests. But he cannot shake off a tense quality, as perceptible as starch.

He says to me one night as we are undressing for bed, 'What do you think is the matter?'

'The matter?'

'With David,' he says, looking down as he takes off his socks.

'He's ill,' I say.

There is a pause.

'Of course he's ill,' Stephen says shortly. 'I asked what you thought the matter was. But never mind.'

With this he lies back and puts off the lamp on his side of the bed. But I am awake for a long time afterward, staring up at a ceiling I can't see in the dark. I don't know what he means by asking me this. Does he believe, because I am his mother, that I should have an inkling of what is happening to David? And should I? Is this fair?

Asking questions, I do fall asleep eventually.

Thus do our lives begin to alter, subtly, imperceptibly, with the change in our midst. We are all of us, in some tiny way, affected.

Except for Moses, who proceeds, oblivious and sulky, with his work. He mows the lawn by the light of the moon and appears not to give a second thought to the people inside the house, clustered like clams about the white bed in which the sick boy lies.

3

David has jaundice. The results of the tests come back and a jubilant Dr Bouch is on the phone, his round voice rolling like a series of little marbles into my ear. He comes out himself later, glowing with pride, as though he is personally responsible for this reverse in our fortunes. He gives David another going-over and confirms this diagnosis. The pain, he tells us, comes from his liver. He leaves him a small bottle of pills.

I walk back out with him to his car. My mother comes with us, hobbling on her crooked feet and clutching Dr Bouch's arm. Her poodle limps behind. She remembers Dr Bouch from the days when he treated her when she first lost her mind. He's kind to her, he smiles.

'Thank you, thank you,' my mother says. She grimaces with delight.

'Only a pleasure, Mrs Roper.' He turns to me and takes my hand. His touch is dry and cool. 'It'll all be over soon,' he says.

This would seem to be true. For a while the jaundice runs its course; there comes into David's complexion a strong yellow colour. He is sick, but not as sick as I'd imagined him to be. So it is with great relief that I observe the illness take effect. His tongue goes yellow. He sweats. His temperature is up and he tosses on the pillow. In a few days I am alarmed to see that the yellow has even coloured his eyes, so that they roll in his head like balls of ivory.

I tend him closely through this time, sitting by him as much as possible.

My absence means that I cannot keep as close an eye elsewhere as I would like. Small duties are neglected. Salome doesn't wash the floor as thoroughly. There are streaks of grime on the window panes. I find traces of soap in the rinsed washing. The bushes in the garden that Moses should be pruning are ragged and badly cut.

I notice these things at night, after David is asleep. Or they are pointed out to me by Stephen, who likes an ordered home. It is he who notices that the bushes aren't properly pruned, one evening as we stroll together in the garden before supper.

'You must keep a firm hand,' he says.

'Yes,' I tell him. 'I'll try.'

It is difficult to do. Watching the servants takes a lot of time. The tasks that have been set for them are a meaningless affair as far as they're concerned. This is not their home. The disciplines of care and cleanliness must be enforced by me. My mother, too, has to be watched, or she will misbehave. She is given to compulsive deeds that are unpleasant and costly. Once I caught her carrying armfuls of books out to a bonfire below the house. Several times she has phoned arbitrary numbers overseas and had long conversations with people on the other side.

I speak to Salome and Moses, scolding them with strong words. They listen but do not respond, standing side by side in the dirt outside the back door. Salome shifts from foot to foot, biting at her lip. Moses, as always, has his eyes fixed on a point behind me and to the left.

I long for this trying time to be over, for things to return to normal. There is a point, it seems, at which life is tedious but most acceptable. We have passed beyond it for a little while, but we will resume our dull course soon. We will be back where we began.

*

But this is not to be, David gets worse, not better. Dr Bouch has been out twice in the last week to examine him and seems happy enough with his recovery. But, as the jaundice goes, it becomes clear to me that something else is taking hold. I watch him carefully.

Now I am afraid. At first I tell myself not to worry. My mind is upset by tensions in the home, but my instinct insists. I look at David one day and see him, with a jarring shock, as a stranger might. How much he's changed. How pale he is, how thin he's getting.

I phone Dr Bouch that night. He sounds peeved, but agrees to drive out. And this time he does not look so calm when he comes out of the room, his little black bag in hand. He walks back with Stephen and me into the lounge, where we all three stand for a long moment without speaking. For some reason the lamps have not been lit in here, and blue light from the moon comes stretching into the room. I am cold, terribly cold, though the air is dense with heat.

Dr Bouch begins. He touches the frame of his spectacles from time to time with a nervous hand.

'There is something,' he says. 'Something …'

A silence falls.

'A growth,' he says. 'In David's throat.'

We look at him. I fumble for Stephen's hand and clench it in my fingers: a limp, a lifeless thing. I let it go.

Dr Bouch continues to speak. He has never seen anything like it. He doesn't know what it is, but he would like me to bring David to the hospital tomorrow. Just for tests. He's sorry to alarm us, but it may, after all, be serious … We are to stay calm.

We do. As we listen to this, standing side by side on the bare lounge floor, I am amazed at how calm we are. It's only

later, after he's gone and we are left, Stephen and I, in the
suddenly brooding house, that panic seizes me. I have a
moment of pure grief, as though David is already gone. I
sway.

Stephen clears his throat. 'Are you all right?' he says.

'Of course I'm not,' I shout. 'Of course I'm not all right!'

I have never shouted at him before. I fall silent again and
we stare at each other. I don't know what he's thinking, but
my head is lurching with a strange and awful liquor.

'There is,' he says, 'no need to scream.'

'I'm sorry,' I begin to say, but he has by now turned
neatly on his heel and left me in the room.

Holding myself, I go to the double doors that lead onto
the back stoep. I push them open and stagger out onto the
blue grass. Stars hang thick and fat, magnified in the clear
air. Under their light I wander to the edge of the lawn and
take the path that leads down below the house.

It's difficult to see in the sticky black, but I push my way
through, tugging at branches, till I come to the cleared acre
where the fruit trees are. They give off a strong smell in the
steamy air, but I don't want to sit. On I go, down, to where,
at the bottom of the cultivated space, the stream is running.
It's only a sound to me in the dark: a constant and stony
gurgling that seems to emerge from the ground. This is
where all our water comes from, pumped up from this
shallow channel in hidden pipes to the house above. I sit
down. My feet find the water and push through it to mud,
oily and black. Cold.

The night is coiled about me like a snake. On the other
side of the stream, invisible to my eyes, the jungle starts: a
wall of vines and trunks that have been woven too tight to
pass. Only sound comes through the leafy chinks: burbling
noises, the pad of paws, the snuffling of breath. Animals are

afoot. We have lost two dogs here, killed by wild pigs. Leopards come down from the mountains sometimes, but they are seldom seen. As I sit now, a wail comes drifting up from the gully. It sounds like a night bird of some kind. Whatever it may be, the noise startles me, plucking a string in me like a ragged nail. I jerk upright, my hair and skin aprickle with fear. It takes a long time before my heart is soft again.

By then I am crying. I couldn't say why. It's not David exactly, but something connected to him. The idea of this growth in him appals me. I see it as an image: a living swelling thing that has bred in his body and that now feeds on him. I see it as a creature with a face. In the gloom, its tiny animal eyes regard me steadily. I cry.

In half an hour I feel better and retrace my steps back up to the house. The lamps have been lit now and Stephen is sitting in the lounge, reading a newspaper. He looks up as I come in.

'Been far?' he says.

'No,' I say. 'Just down to the stream.'

'Ah.' He nods. After a moment he looks back down at his paper. I know that all is well, that things are better between us. We have, by silent consent, agreed through the ten years of our marriage never to raise our voices to each other. We do disagree on occasion, but only with quiet tones and rational argument. Though we haven't, as I say, discussed it, Stephen would consider any display of emotion unnecessary. I have, till now, honoured his wishes. Tonight I have been silly. I have overstepped myself.

But it's all right now. I gather myself and walk on down the passage to David's room, to tell him what is to happen tomorrow.

I take him to the hospital. This is a small building at the

edge of town and not, by city standards, what it claims to be. It's more a clinic than anything else: a dirty white building with three frayed palm trees outside. A fat nurse takes down my name and address and shows me where to wait.

Soon afterwards, we are shown into a consulting room very like Dr Bouch's in town. Dr Bouch is here, together with two other doctors. Their names are Viljoen and Van Zyl. Once again, David must undress and lie down on the white table. The three men crowd about him, probing him like plump white bees at a flower. This time they are not concerned with the surface of his body. It's his throat into which they are peering, aiming their tiny torches like guns. They mutter among themselves, speaking a language I cannot understand.

Eventually they call me over, and I too am given a chance to look down the gullet of my son at what is living there. I peer down, afraid. It's an innocuous thing, this growth; not at all what I imagined. Tiny and red and almost harmless, like a small sea creature trapped where it does not belong.

Dr Bouch is talking to me. I tear my eyes away, reluctant, '... to be done,' he is saying. 'There are decisions to be made.'

'Yes,' I say, unsure of what he means.

'For now, he must be kept in bed. I'll come up every day. I'll write out some prescriptions for you. We must try various methods.'

'Yes,' I say. I smile at him.

'There isn't necessarily any cause for alarm.' This from Dr Viljoen, who is holding my wrist with a tender grip, as if he is taking my pulse.

'Yes.'

'Good, then. Good.'

And we are being ushered from the room, David still doing up the buttons of his shirt. The fat nurse smiles as we go out.

I go to the chemist and obtain, with the prescription, assortments of pills in bottles. I regard these in the same way I do the other pills Dr Bouch had left us. I suppose it is mistrust. I suppose, yes, it is still as mild as that: mistrust for these coloured objects in their transparent containers that are meant to cure and heal.

I discuss this with Stephen that night. He looks at me, surprised.

'But of course he must take them,' he says. 'If that's what Dr Bouch told you.'

'But he doesn't know what's wrong with him. How can he prescribe medicines when he doesn't know what's wrong?'

'You're being silly,' he tells me. 'He has a job to do. Let him do his job.'

'I have a job too,' I say. 'I must take care of David. I must do the best I can for him.'

We drop the subject then, but there is a tension between us that hasn't been there before. I sit with David for a while. Then I go to bed.

4

David is dying. I know this fact long before it is confirmed for me on a certain morning by Dr Bouch. On this morning, after examining David, Dr Bouch takes me to the corner of the lounge to which we always withdraw and says:

'He must go to hospital.'

I look at him.

'I mean,' he says, 'a proper hospital. We haven't the facilities here to deal with this case. There is nothing more I can do for him.'

'What are you saying?'

'I am saying,' he tells me, looking me in the eye, 'I am saying that you must take him to the city.'

The city. The words strike in me like a heavy iron clapper, sending out echoes in images of tall dirty buildings, streets as deep as rivers, cars, windows, noise. I lived in the city when I was training to be a teacher. I cannot bear the thought of it.

'No,' I say.

'I'm afraid he must. I don't know if you understand. He *has* to go.'

'No,' I say again, though my voice is trembling.

Dr Bouch stares at me. A kind of silent antagonism has developed between us, over the mornings and mornings that he has been here and been able to tell me nothing. He peers into every crevice of David's body, but cannot discover what is wrong. The most he's been able to find out, to my horror and fright, is that the growth in his throat is getting bigger every day. He reminds me of this now.

'It's doubling in size,' he says, 'every twenty-four hours.'

I look steadily back at him, though my heart beats at my chest like a fist.

'I am warning you,' he says, opening his hands to me.

Again I shake my head. A silence falls. Then he bends to his bag and prepares to leave. He mutters angrily as he does: 'All right. The choice is yours. I'll come back tomorrow. But I told you ...'

He told me. But I do not tell Stephen when he comes home that night; nor any night after. My silence in this matter is not an easy one. I am ridden with guilt afterwards. I know full well that in the city there are better and brighter men than these, men who may be able to discover what it is that is devouring David from inside. It is fear that prevents me from agreeing, that bends my lips into their resilient shape.

I am selfish. I am small. My life has devolved to numberless small routines that keep me safe. I trust my existence in this place, with its small population of inhabitants. I recoil at the thought of the city, of giving up, even for a time, the secure arrangement of home and husband and servants that rings me round.

But David is dying. I spend most of every day with him now in his room. He no longer laughs or talks very much. I read to him, but he listens with listless boredom, staring with glassy eyes into the distance. He lies very still. Too still sometimes: I have stopped rigid with shock at least twice when coming into the room and seeing him like that. When he does move, it is with stiff slowness, as if his joints are hardening. He cries often: small whimpering sobs that jerk from his mouth.

I watch, amazed. How swiftly it happens. I count the days since this began, since that first afternoon he came to me, and think how, in this measured space of time, the complex perfect knots that bind up his body are undoing themselves, one after the other. There is a seam in him that is unravelling, somewhere in the deep dark places under the sheets that cover him. I can't reach there with hand or prayer.

I watch him go. Each day, each hour perhaps, the rot keeps on, advancing by slow degrees until the moment it will consume him. I no longer cry over him. Impossibly, I have become used to this. I have accepted into the ordinary patterns of my hours this most extraordinary thing. As have we all: Salome and Moses, no longer under my will, work where and when they please. I notice only, on my journeys to the kitchen or outside, that all is not as it was. The grass is too long. The fat summer petals are strewn under the trees. Inside, the floors grow dull. Dust collects in corners and against skirting boards.

There are moments when I react with outrage and fury. At these times I lose control: I fly out in search of these two, my hair wild. 'Salome!' I call. 'Moses!' If they reply, I round them up and lecture them, berating them in high, shrill tones, telling them how they are letting me down. But they are immune, it seems, to my rages: they merely stand, unblinking, while I expend my breath.

Finally I give up this ritual. It has no effect and wastes my time. Besides, there seems no point, when there are no guests or friends to entertain. Even Stephen makes no mention of it anymore, though I know that it bothers him.

Stephen has become quieter as the days go by. He was never a talkative man, but now, even in our most intimate moments alone, he hardly speaks. He avoids my eyes. At night, after the servants and doctors are gone, a dreadful silence falls on the house, through which he and I move like anguished ghosts. Only the solemn monotonous ticking of the clock spreads in concentric rings from its place in the lounge, paring away our lives.

There are times, yes, when we speak. But, strangely, we talk little of David. It's everyday matters, trivial concerns, that are the subject of our discussion. 'We must fill the gas-lamps,' he might say. 'They're about to run out.'

Or: 'I saw a shirt today I like. I think I might buy it.'

If David is seldom mentioned, it's because we cannot agree. We, who in ten years of marriage have never had cause for real dispute, find ourselves in opposition over something we do not understand. We have argued over him: over the pills he takes, over what is the matter and how to deal with it. In these arguments it is I who become passionate, I who scream and point. Once I banged my head with force against the wall. Stephen merely studies me with icy reserve, observing me as he does the boys who are sent to his office to be punished. I am an object to him at times like these; an irrational, emotional being who cannot command herself. I think he feels distaste.

He is away most of the day, though, and is spared the relentless process that is taking place. It is I who spend my days in the tiny room, sitting at the bedside and passing the hours. My mother still comes to join us there, but she is not as talkative as before. For one thing, David is hardly interested in conversation anymore. But I value her presence now, why I cannot say. It's a comfort to me to have her there, an older, dimmer version of myself, a reminder to me of what I may become.

It's not just weakness that makes David quiet: among the pills that I reluctantly feed him is a drug that lessens the pain he feels. But this drug also slows him down, wrapping his mind in bandages I cannot penetrate. He speaks thickly (when he does), as if his tongue is made of wool.

He sweats. I draw the curtains in the room. As time goes by, there is more to tending him, and the hours are not as dull. He bleeds from every orifice, tiny private trickles of blood that stain the sheet. He bleeds from his ears, his nose. When he goes to the toilet, which he does very seldom and only with my help, the water is full of blood. He even, toward the end, begins to bleed from his eyes. This, more than anything that has gone before, reaches me in a terrible way. I stare, numb with horror, as thick red tears well up at the corners of his eyes and move slowly over his cheeks.

But I clean the sheets. I change his linen daily and air the room. I help him to the bathroom and wash him. As he becomes weaker, I wash him in bed with a flannel and a tub of water. I bring him food, which he chews with difficult movements of his jaw. It hurts him to swallow and to talk.

I think of the growth in his throat as a ghastly crimson plant, inching up towards the light. It has reached tentacles into his nose, his ears, the sockets behind his eyes. So, the blood. He does not seem alarmed at the progress of this foreign presence he must be able to sense in himself. Perhaps he doesn't care. When he tries to talk, the words are blurred by the choked hole of his neck. Often I cannot understand what he says. On occasions I find myself shouting at him.

'Speak properly!' I say. 'Express yourself.'

I'm not a patient woman, but I hate myself for these outbursts against what he cannot help. I hug him afterwards and tell him I'm sorry. Often, without warning to either of us, I burst into tears. It is he who consoles me then, patting at my shoulder with a spidery hand.

'Don't cry,' he says. 'I don't want you to cry.'

I can't explain to him why I do, or what is happening to him. He knows only that he's sick. This he accepts, along with the assumption that he will be well again. We discuss it no further between us, though I dread the questions he could ask.

I think he's too occupied, however, with the business of enduring. I cannot imagine what it is he's undergoing, far below the surface of himself. It must take great resources of spirit to resist this onslaught that never lets up, minute to minute to minute. As I am concerned with my own survival, so must he be with his. I can do nothing to help him, as he can do nothing for me. We have, both of us, been put under siege by a force far stronger than ourselves. We can but wait.

He suffers. The pain that began as a twinge has grown in him till now it has overflowed his body and, I dare say, reaches far beyond the house. I see it sometimes as almost a tangible thing: a kind of light that burns out of his face. It flickers around the bed. For reasons I don't understand, this pain seems worst at night. It builds in him till he doesn't know what to do with it. Then I watch as, a translucent skeletal figure, he stands up out of bed and begins to dance about the room. He dashes himself against objects, against walls and tables. He tears at his hair. Huge liquid moans rise from him in bubbles, floating up and bursting loudly against the roof. He does ridiculous things. He tears his clothes. He pulls down his pants and pulls them up again. He wrenches himself from side to side, wiping snot and tears across his mouth, braying and calling, gnashing and swearing. All this – this helpless, hopeless activity – to ward off the nerves in his body.

There is nothing at these times that I or medicine can do for him. It happens so often, with such regularity, that his dance ceases to move me. I sit silently by in the deep armchair and watch him as he cavorts back and forth, to and fro. Once or twice I cannot contain my frustration; I tear at my own hair; I shout. 'Stop!' I say. 'You're driving me crazy! Please stop and lie down.' He doesn't hear or obey.

But eventually he lies again. Drenched with sweat, gasping with exhaustion, still twitching with sharp flashes from within, he sprawls on the bed. Holding the sheet in his fists and between his teeth, he falls asleep.

In the end, I move into the room. I cannot bear to abandon him here each night and return to my own room next door, where my husband lies waiting. I experience each morning a feeling of dread as I get up, head buzzing with fatigue, and stagger back through to David. One night, unbeknown to me, he will stop breathing while I am asleep. If this is to happen, I would want to be there.

I tell Stephen. 'I'm going to ask Moses to move the spare bed in.'

Unexpectedly, he glares at me. We are sitting in the kitchen, at the breakfast table, where I have cooked for him before he goes to work. 'And me?' he says.

'What do you mean?' I blink, surprised.

'I mean that I hardly see you anymore. You spend your time, all your time, in that room. What do you think you can do all night? Can you save his life?'

'Don't speak like that to me.' My voice has come out of me far higher and sharper than I intended. We stare at each other over the table, while the room rocks about us.

'I am tired of this,' he says in a low and threatening voice. 'I don't know how much you think I can put up with. You are not the only person in this house –'

'And nor are you.' I am standing before I know it, lashing out with my arms. I catch the plate of egg before him and it flies, it breaks. He is sitting, staring at me, while

I give in to myself. I seize the pitcher of orange juice and throw it to the floor. I fling the knives, the forks. 'That is your son,' I scream. 'Do you think I want him ill? Do you think I made things this way?'

He also stands now, so that we are facing each other eye to eye. He leans towards me, balancing a fist on the table.

'Dr Bouch called me,' he says. 'He told me he asked you to take David to hospital.'

'Yes?' I say. I'm gasping now as I cry. I smooth down my hair.

'Why didn't you tell me?' he says.

'Because it doesn't matter. Because he isn't going. I don't believe in what they're going to do to him. Stephen,' I say, shaking my head, 'Stephen, Stephen.'

He looks at me for a long long time. Then he slowly straightens and goes out of the room.

That night he tells me he's sorry. We're standing on the back stoep, looking out on the forest that falls away below us. The moon is up, a bowl of light.

'The strain is getting to me,' he says.

'It's all right,' I tell him. 'I'm sorry too.'

But we do not touch as we stand, facing out towards the moon over the low tops of the trees. There is a chill in the air. I am chilled, too, by this moment of raw honesty which we have never been capable of before. I discover for the first time that Stephen has feelings.

Nevertheless, I have had the spare bed moved into David's room. My vigil, now, extends into the dark. There is no longer such a thing as day or night in the narrow room: it's easy to be unaware of what takes place outside. I am always here; I go out only to the toilet and bath and for the occasional breath of air. Otherwise I sit or stand or lie within reach of the bed, trying to combat what my body demands: I force myself to stay awake. Even when David has fallen asleep I recite rhymes to myself, pinch my thighs, to keep from blacking out. I watch over him.

In this dreadful time, this most solitary of confinements, I become intimate with every detail of the room. I notice things I have never noticed before: the fraying edge of the coverlet, faces in the wallpaper. A tiny crack in the windowsill where ants are nesting. My mind roams over these things in search of escape, but must, in the end, turn inward.

To me, and what I contain. A communication develops between David and myself that is not based on words. He moves his third finger when he wants water. He rolls his eyes when he needs to piss. I respond to these calls, aiding the functions of his body in their task of keeping him alive. But my mind, trapped in this stillness, draws up from itself a constant stream of images from the past. I see David as a baby. My tired brown nipple is in his mouth. I teach him to walk. I teach him how to use the toilet. Questions follow these images: have I been a good mother to him? Have I given him what he needs? What unknowable damages have I committed in my laziness, my ignorance? What? What? I shake my head to clear the web of words.

The questions sing upon the air.

Beyond this room, other lives, like satellites, continue in their orbit. I see Stephen from time to time, when he comes into the room after work, or sits with us for a while before bed. Salome still makes meals (mashed food now, all that David can swallow) and brings them in. I see Moses, and sometimes my mother, as they walk past the window outside. But these people are strange to me, like friends remembered from long ago. They don't touch in any real way on my existence here, on David's, in the tiny space between these four walls. They go about a separate business to us, not knowing, as we do, how sordid a thing this waiting is, how wearisome this agony.

Stephen now does the shopping. He eats alone at the table in the evenings, waited upon by Salome, who has been asked to stay late. There was a time when we would all eat together, assembled in uncomfortable silence in one corner of the kitchen. I suppose it's a blessing to be free of obligations like these. Now, after eating, Stephen comes through and joins me. He sits on the opposite side of the bed, leaning forward in his chair, hands between his knees. Neither of us speaks, to each other or to David. (David can barely talk anymore, his throat is too small.) In silence we sit, glancing at each other now and then, with the huge white bed between us.

Dr Bouch comes to visit in the mornings. I have little to say to him. Since he phoned Stephen without my knowledge, my fury for him is unbridled. I grunt if he speaks to me, but he has nothing to offer, no new insights to surprise me. He comes each morning, looks into David's mouth, and departs soon after, shrugging as he goes.

I too am ill. My mouth is sore, full of little white blisters that have come out on my tongue and gums. I itch. The room is hazy about me now, seen through eyes filmed over with blood. Perhaps, if I will myself to it, I shall crack and die before David does. But I don't think so: there is that in me which shall go on, and go on, and go on. I know too well.

I hear a wailing from outside. Leaning against the wall, I go out to the door and see, in the middle of the lawn, the white corpse of my mother's dog. She stands over it, wrenching her hands.

'Ohh,' she cries. 'Look what's happened now.'

I go to her across the lawn, unbalanced in the blinding sun. The dog is lying on its side, tongue sticking stiff and pink from its mouth. Fleas are jumping off its cooling skin. I take my mother by the hand.

'He won't get up,' she cries. 'Make him get up.'

I take her inside. I tell Moses to bury the animal in the forest and I lead my stricken mother back with me to the room. She quietens quickly, forgetting soon the dreadful silence of the wretched white beast. But I, strangely, can not: for the first time in many weeks I begin to cry. Tears force their way from me, pushing up like lava through tunnels clenched shut. I sob into my hand, firing my grief like a gun. She watches me, composed, as I mourn the passing of that limping poodle as I do my life, the farm, my child, the man I married.

Then I get up and close the curtains.

'Pooh,' says my mother. 'It smells in here.'

It does. A stale stench is on the air: the fumes of sweat and blood and bile. It's hard to breathe.

The days go by. *Let it end*, I think. *Let it end*.

But it doesn't end. It just keeps on, spinning out like a tale without a theme. I wait and wait and wait, till it seems I have heard no other sound in forty-two years than the dragging wheeze of David trying to draw breath.

I go in search of the other doctor. Late one night, after Stephen has gone to bed and David has finally fallen asleep, I stand up and leave the house. I move over the quietly prickling lawn, past the doorway to my mother's rooms where she is also standing, torch in hand, staring at the sky. She watches me as I go, but doesn't call out. I make my way down the grass-edged drive to the iron gate all wound about with vines and step out into the cool dust road that runs under the trees. I stand there for a moment. The night is still.

I pass over the road and onto the bare path that runs up toward the tops of the mountains. I know the way because I've walked it before. I begin to climb.

Though I have looked for him before without success, I've never tried at night. He must have a fire, I tell myself, by which I will track him down. I will see the light, like a little red window, shining from his cave.

But there is no fire. I walk and walk till I am gasping and falling, and my dress is full of thorns. The path trails out and I leave it behind. I climb through the jungled trees like an ape; like a creature on the hunt. The other night animals going about their ways are startled by me. They stop and stare from a distance, hooding their burning eyes, as I go past.

Perhaps he too has heard me approach. Perhaps he too has doused his fire and is standing at the mouth of his cave, hands on hips, watching with interest as I stagger by. Or perhaps he doesn't exist after all, never has, except in the cave of my head. I have paid tribute to him there often enough: knelt before him in his skins and beads, with bone-throwing hands.

When I am too tired to go farther I stop and look down the valley. All is in darkness: the gorges, the gullies, the slopes of trees; except for where, far, far below, the town softly glimmers in a puddle of light. Our house is invisible from here. I turn and go back.

I arrive home aching and bruised. My mother is standing in the same place she was when I left, the torch still flickering dimly in her hand. She watches me as I go by.

I pack our bags and I take David to the city.

TWO

5

It is extraordinary, after all, how swiftly one adjusts. What I had dreaded most about a life in the city was the establishment of routine, but within a day (a few days, perhaps) I have become accustomed to the way things work. Nothing, in the end, has changed very much. I continue to spend my time at the side of David's bed. As before, I read to him or talk. From time to time other people enter, but now it's no longer my mother, or Salome bearing trays of food. Strangers come in to tend to David. They treat me kindly, these people, all of them dressed in white. They are doctors and nurses, gliding across the smooth-tiled floor like religious visions.

If anything, it's easier for me here. I no longer have to wash David, or feed him, or take him to the toilet. There are other people to do these things for me, professional people whose job it is to care for the sick. It is up to me only to sit by him and be his mother.

It is a pleasant room. The walls are painted a gentle blue, the curtains are white. There is very little in here, other than the bed and the chair on which I like to sit. There is a cupboard, but it is empty.

When David sleeps, which he does often, I like to look out of the window at the streets below. I can see buildings from up here, biting into the sky like teeth.

It's a hard place, this city, and I am afraid of it. Things move here more swiftly than I am used to. Cars surge in the streets. People jostle and push on the pavements. When I walk home or in town, I keep close to the edges of buildings so as not to be in the way.

But in here it is different. In the quiet interior of the ward there is no hint of the frenzy outside. People pass. This is a world populated by strange and curious beasts: men in pyjamas, in wheelchairs, women in bathrobes, on stretchers. There is a sharp singeing smell to everything. Voices are soft, playing in the background like relaxing music. I don't know much about these other people, and I have spoken to few of them. There is, I know, another small boy at the end of the passage whose mother comes to visit him. His name is Jason. His mother's name is Sarah. She seizes me one day in the corridor, her eyes round as bullet-holes, her mouth working. 'You're the ...' she gasps, 'the other ...'

'Yes,' I say. 'I am.'

'I am so sorry. I know, believe me, how it feels.'

'Yes?' I stare at her, alarmed.

'We must,' she says, 'get together for tea. And talk.'

'All right,' I say, and she lets me go. But in truth I have no desire to meet her over tea. I think we have nothing to say to each other.

I ask David if he knows Jason.

'No,' he says. 'I never get out of bed.'

This is so: he must lie as he is, moving only from side to side. In two months now he has not taken a single step.

'Would you like to meet him? Would that be nice?'

'No.' He pulls a face. David is shy, and dislikes other boys.

'He's also sick,' I urge him. 'He's also lonely.'

'I'm not lonely.' His lip is trembling. I become impatient, but control myself in time.

'How do you feel?' I ask.

'Okay.'

His voice is tinny, like the voice of a ghost. To speak he

must cover the hole in his throat with one hand, or all the air comes hissing out.

'Why is the hole here?'

'So that you can breathe.'

'How did they make it?'

'With a knife.'

'Did you watch them do it?'

'No.'

'Did it bleed?'

'I suppose it must have.'

All these questions. I smile. I suppose I should be grateful to see him this way, a resurrected version of himself. But I have been told over and over by Professor Terry that I must not raise my hopes.

Professor Terry is the man I have travelled all this way to find: a substitute for Dr Bouch. He is large, built like a construction worker rather than a physician. His hands, too, are brutal and big. But his face is delicate, made of fine bones. It's the face of a pure man; clean-shaven, smooth-skinned, pale. He wears glasses when he reads. He has grey hair oiled down perfectly like a cap.

It is Professor Terry who has explained to me the nature and course of my son's disease. I listen, intrigued and dismayed, to what dreadful events were taking place in his body while I sat by. The cells, Professor Terry explains, go mad. They divide and reproduce endlessly, out of control. I shift in my seat, unnerved at this description of nature gone berserk.

'Do you have any questions?' he says then, smiling kindly.

'Yes,' I say. 'If you don't mind.'

'Not at all. Please go ahead.'

I ask. He answers.

It's a rare form of the disease, he tells me. Nobody is exactly sure what causes it, but that is beside the point. The point is that there are four stages to the disease, and David has entered the fourth and final stage.

'You must not raise your hopes,' the professor says. 'I'm afraid that there is very little chance.'

He speaks directly. Perhaps because my senses have been blunted over the many days past, his words have little effect. I lean forward and say:

'There is a chance.'

He considers me gravely. He is a busy man.

'David is still very, very sick,' he says. 'You must remember that. The operation has removed the growth, but it has not contained the illness. The illness is everywhere. Everywhere. You must bear that in mind.'

I bear it in mind. I know these facts: his body is full of cells that are multiplying without cause. This condition has spread from his glands to his brain. His liver is eighteen times its normal size and two per cent functioning. He is thinner than a thong.

'What can you do for him?' I ask.

'We are giving him treatment.'

The first time I hear this word, it is with relief. I am prepared to give in to these men in white coats, to allow them their way with their pills and their needles.

I go in to the hospital twice a day: for two hours in the morning and two in the afternoon. That is all I am allowed. During the rest of the day I wander in town, I go shopping. In the evenings I return to where I sleep, which is at the home of Stephen's sister and her husband. Her name is Linda. His name is Glenn.

Linda is as tall as Stephen, but where his hair is rough and dark, hers is fine and white. Her skin is covered with blemishes and freckles, marked like a surface on which stains have formed. There is a gap between her two front teeth through which her tongue gleams pink. She is a nervous woman, always changing position and touching at her face with long, unpainted nails. She wears slacksuits and belts with flat shoes, under which her body seems even thinner than it is.

'You must be so worn out,' she cries. 'My dear.'

Like the rest of her, her voice is reedy and dull. I have never liked her much. I don't know her well, as she and Glenn come up to see us only over Christmas. But I can't bring myself to trust her now, with her pleas of sympathy, her offers of help.

'Anything,' she says. 'Anything, my dear, that you might need.'

'Yes,' says Glenn. 'You have only to ask.'

He is a short man, and overweight. He is a journalist by profession and wears journalists' clothes: casual, colourless, neat. His pouchy face wobbles as he talks, pushing out words like little puffs of smoke. I have no reason for believing so, but I suspect he treats Linda badly.

'Thank you,' I say. 'It's very good of you.'

'Not at all, my dear ...'

'It's only a pleasure,' says Glenn, shaking his head.

They live in a flat close to the city centre. It's not a large flat, but is equipped, Linda explains, with everything they need. I am given a key of my own.

My room is blue and pink, with a white carpet on the floor. There is a bathroom next door. From my window I have a view of a large park in the adjoining block, full of gravel drives and trees.

I go for walks in this park in the long evenings, with the light dying overhead — so much more easily than we. The shadows gather, clotting like blue blood under trees and fountains, spilling out. There is a statue in the middle of the park, cast in iron: the figure of a man I have not heard of, who stands in stiff, ungainly clothes, staring out into the gloom. Pigeons roost beneath his hat.

How strangely and how much my life has changed. There are moments now when I reflect on all that has taken place and like a woman asleep, I jerk to my senses, amazed. Nothing is the way it was. All that I had taken for granted has been pulled out from under me like a mat. My home – the house built of stones and straw – is far away from here, so far that I can only imagine it.

Stephen is there. He drove down to be with me when he heard about the operation, but has since gone back. There is work to be done, he explains. He has a school to run. I feel sorry for Stephen, who has no choice, but I miss him enough to be angry with him. He phones me each night and the sound of his voice provokes me to tears.

'Don't cry,' he says. 'I know it's hard.'

'It's easy on you,' I say. 'I'm the one who has to be here, watching … If you only knew what they're doing to him …'

'I know. Of course I know. But what else can I do?'

It has become possible for us to snap. Even Stephen, in his tight blue suits, is given to irritation these days. We are not what we were.

'I'm sorry,' he says. 'It's difficult for both of us.'

'Stephen,' I say, and I start to cry again. 'I want to come home. I want this to be over.'

'It will be over,' he says, 'soon enough.'

Over weekends, when he can, he drives down to be with me. We sleep together then in my blue and pink room in Linda's flat. These are awkward times for me, with Linda bobbing around her brother like a frightened moth.

'Poor Stephen,' she says. 'What a terrible strain. Back and forth.'

It is a long way, but he doesn't, I think, resent the trip. It is five hours in the car; five hours that bring him to David and to me. But Linda's pity puts questions in my head: am I a burden to him? Does he begrudge me his time?

I ask him.

'Of course not,' he says. 'How can you think that?'

'I just wondered.'

He comes to me and takes my face in his hands. He looks into my eyes. 'You don't look well,' he says. 'You need a rest.'

'I know,' I say. Before I can help it, I begin to cry again. I am so ashamed of these tears, over which it seems I have no control. 'I'm sorry,' I say.

'Why don't you take a break? Why don't you go away?'

'And David? What about him? What will he do while I'm away and there is no one, no one, to be with him?'

He doesn't reply. There is nothing to say.

When Stephen is here, we go in together to visit David.

My heart lurches at the way he smiles when he catches sight of his father. I am jealous, I admit, of his delight. Things are easier between them now than ever before. Distance and pain have made them warm to each other. Stephen takes his hand and they talk.

'How are you doing, big boy?' says Stephen.

'Fine,' says David. 'But they hurt me.'

'It's the only way to make you better.'

'I know. But it's sore.'

'You must be a big brave boy,' says Stephen. 'For me. For your father.'

They grin, conspiring.

While he is here, Stephen makes a point of seeing Professor Terry. They get on well, these two, in the way of professional men. They shake hands and talk over the vast surface of the desk that stands in the professor's office.

'Can you give me an idea of how he's responding to the treatment?' Stephen asks, fingers steepled under his chin.

'Well, Stephen,' the professor says, blowing out his cheeks. 'It's difficult to say. The drugs are very powerful, but it's early days yet. Early days. As I have told your wife, you must not raise your hopes.'

'I understand,' says Stephen pleasantly. He rises to go. 'I'm afraid we must be off.'

'Goodbye, Stephen. See you next weekend.'

I remember for a long time afterwards, and with bitterness, how pleasantly Stephen accepted that he should not raise his hopes.

We are, of course, all of us under pressure. Never before in our lives have we had to contend with such things as dispute and separation. But it occurs to me, as it has before, that my husband is not the person I believed him to be.

The treatment of which Professor Terry spoke is a complicated business. Each morning, at a certain hour, a Dr Tredoux comes into the room, followed by two nurses pushing a metal trolley. On this trolley are instruments of various kinds and bowls of steaming water. Dr Tredoux is a friendly man. With great bravura he enters, grinning broadly, rolling up his sleeves. 'How are we today?' he booms, as if all of us are suffering together. He goes to the tap to wash his hands, humming as he does some mindless, silly tune. The nurses close on David. They take his pulse, his temperature. They ruffle his hair. Despite these signs of friendliness, David is not deceived. He looks at me with wildly rolling eyes, holding his breath. Eventually he begins to cry.

'What's this, what's this?' Dr Tredoux advances on the bed till he looms whitely over us, big as an angel. 'We're not frightened, are we? Of a little pain?'

David doesn't answer. His hand grips mine like the jaws of a dog.

They unbutton and remove David's pyjama top. Then, still humming, as unconcerned as if he is making himself a sandwich, Dr Tredoux prepares a syringe. He takes it from a sealed plastic bag. He inserts a needle. One of the nurses ties a piece of rubber tubing about David's upper arm. The other stands opposite me on the other side of the bed. She looks at me and smiles.

'Shame,' she whispers.

For a moment I'm not sure who she is referring to: me or David. But he is the more obvious subject for compassion. I look down to see what has, once again, become too normal: a little boy in bed, terribly thin, except for the distended bulge that is his liver. His ribs stand out. His skin is grey. The hole in his throat is taped over with gauze. A drip stands beside me, attached by a long pipe to a needle in his hand.

'There now,' crackles Dr Tredoux. 'That wasn't so bad.'

And I see that he has finished his first task. The syringe is bright with blood. As I watch, he plucks it out like a thorn. The flesh clings, lets go.

Then the next. It is this syringe that David eyes with shivering fear. He rolls away from it in the bed, grabbing at me. 'Don't let them,' he says. 'Don't let them.' But I have no choice: with the nurses, I push him back into the pillow.

Dr Tredoux inserts the needle. He pushes the plunger, sending the column of yellow fluid into David's arm. It's over in a moment and the needle is withdrawn. I know very little about the nature of this drug: only that it kills the cells that cause the anarchy. Professor Terry has explained. But in so doing, he tells me, it will kill many healthy cells too. David will lose his hair. He will be sick.

'The price we pay,' he says, throwing up his hands.

David begins to vomit. Two seconds, perhaps, after the injection is done, he tells me he can feel it reach his tongue: a taste like rot. And he hunches over in the bed, convulsing with the effort of emptying his body, trying to rid it of this poison. I clutch him. One of the nurses, well trained, is holding a bowl to catch the load. He heaves, shuddering. I raise my eyes to those of Dr Tredoux, who looks steadily back at me, neutral and cool.

The bowl is removed, placed back on the trolley. I touch David's head to make him look at me, to remind him I am here and on his side. But he doesn't look up. Greyer than before, blubbering slightly, he falls back over the pillows as if he has been punctured by that needle.

But there is another to come. This is the largest of them all: a syringe as thick as a wrist, a needle as long as a pencil. The nurses seize David. They put over his head a small white jacket that has, at the back, a circular hole cut out of its centre. They roll him on his side so that he faces me. 'Now curl up,' says one of the nurses. 'Come on. It'll be over in a second.'

'The quicker you are, the quicker it'll be done.' Dr Tredoux flashes a glance at me: an appeal. But I do not flinch. I stare him down.

'Come, David,' the other nurse says.

Because David is howling like a wolf and rolling in the bed. He grabs at me again. Finally I cannot stand it anymore and I put out my hand. 'David,' I say, 'you must.'

He subsides, snivelling. There is a fleck of foam at the corner of his mouth. As if he is a dummy, the nurses roll him back onto his side with his knees up against his tummy. He is a foetal shape, the outline of my womb.

We hold him down. The nurses and I, leaning with our weight, pin him in this position to the bed. ('It is very dangerous,' Professor Terry has said. 'He must not move.') Dr Tredoux, aiming carefully, presses the needle against his spine where it stands out in a ridge in the circular hole in the jacket. Then, a knife into butter, he pushes it in. As it slides, David screams: a sound, primeval, released. It hits me there too, at the base of my spine. They draw fluid out, sucking it carefully from the slender white stalk that holds up his body. Then they inject fluid in. And all the time my son is screaming.

Then it is over. The nurses are putting away the needles and pans. They take the jacket. Dr Tredoux wipes his hands on the white lapels of his coat. 'There,' he says. 'It wasn't so bad.'

I find myself saying: 'Thank you.'

They go. For a long time afterwards, David doesn't move. He continues to lie on his side with his knees drawn up, sobbing hoarsely as though with grief. I don't know how to console him, or if I want to. I run my hands over him, pressing gently at the spongy texture of his flesh. 'David,' I say. 'I'm sorry, I'm sorry.'

'I have to vomit again,' he says.

They've left a bowl beside the bed. I hold it for him as he retches. He shudders, then falls back again, an arm across his face as he cries and cries and cries.

Every day this happens.

I go to see Professor Terry in his office. He receives me with a tired but patient air, as if he recognises me for what I am: a meddler, a busy-body.

'Of course the treatment is necessary,' he says. 'You don't think we do if for pleasure, do you?'

'No. But I wonder if there isn't some other way – '

'Everybody wonders that,' he says. 'We all wonder that every day. Research,' he tells me, 'is continuing.'

There is only one other thing I need to know. 'How long must the treatment go on?'

'If it is successful,' he says, leaning forward, 'he must keep coming back for ten years.'

'Ten years?' I repeat, lame in my chair as I stare at him.

'I'm afraid so. To be on the safe side.'

The interview is over.

Ten years, I know already, is too long a time for either of us to endure. David is my son. He has been in me more deeply and more intimately than any lover I've had. We undergo this attrition together.

6

It is at some time now, while we are living this way with so much distance and time between us, that betrayal begins. I have no thoughts, no profound understandings to offer. Perhaps the sickness in our midst makes deception easier to practise. I prefer to think, however, that we begin to see each other honestly, and cannot bear what we see. At any rate, I have no warning. I think back over the weekends that Stephen has spent with me here. I remember the phone calls he's made, but find no clue to what is taking place.

The first I learn of it is when I receive a call one evening after returning from the hospital. I am greeted with a slow, strange breathing on the other side.

'Hello?' I say.

'Do you know,' a voice informs me (a woman's voice, muffled and high), 'that your husband is having an affair?'

'What?' I say, unsure whether I've heard correctly. But there is only a silence before the line goes dead.

I am suddenly weak. Shock falls over me like a blinding white dome in which I am moving, silent and bereft.

Linda is concerned. She follows after me, tugging at my arm. 'What?' she cries. 'Was it the hospital? Is it David?' When I continue to ignore her, she can no longer resist. 'Has it happened?' she says.

'No,' I say. 'It isn't that.'

The next day, sick and sleepless, I pack my bag. I tell Linda that I must go home. 'To settle some matters,' I say. She twitters consent, but I can tell by the way she looks at me from her frightened grey eyes that she knows something is wrong.

Before I leave, I go to the hospital to tell David I shall be away for a day. He accepts the news without concern, but when Dr Tredoux, on his daily rounds, inserts the second needle into his arm, he releases a thin high wail I've never heard from him before. We cling to each other with tiny mammal hands, the sick boy (my child) and I. The sound of his cry is in tune with something in me, so that for a moment we sing out together: high, lonely, and in pain.

I get back home in the late afternoon, with the shadows of the trees stretched long and pale across the grass. It is strange to see the house again after being away for so long. There is no sign of anybody. A pelt of dust is on the floor. 'Salome!' I call. 'Moses!' But there is no reply.

I sit down to wait in the lounge, in the large armchair at the window. The gas-lamps are unlit, and the shadows deepen about me as the evening comes on. There is no sound from inside the house, except for the occasional squeak or fart of rafters. Outside, the air buzzes gently with birds and insects.

Eventually, I hear the noise of Stephen's bakkie from far down the road, long before it comes into view, trundling across the grass and out of sight again around the corner. Before, when all was well, I used to go out to greet him when he came home. But not tonight. He must see my car when he parks his, but he doesn't hurry. In fact it is a long time before I hear the tread of his footsteps on the lawn and he appears on the stoep, walking slow and stiff, trailing on the air like smoke.

It's twilight now. A blue darkness has welled up from the ground, drifting like fine spray into the air. He comes to a stop in the doorway, leaning disjointedly against it as he would never have done in time gone by. We look at each other, silent, across the shadow-scarred boards of the floor. And I see, yes, that he too has had a vigil to keep up, alone in the house with its walls of stone, filling up with darkness as with water.

'Hello, Stephen.'

'Hello,' he says, and at last tears loose from the jamb, comes staggering across the floor towards me. He sits in the chair beside me, his knee bumping against mine. He pulls it away.

Through the five interminable hours of travel, I have thought of a great many things to ask or say. Bitter accusations filled my head. But now I find there is nothing to discuss. Perhaps we are finally tired, he and I, after the tedious months gone by. Perhaps we have realised that words are for the young and eager.

When we do, eventually, talk, it is about matters of no consequence.

'The drive ... ?' he says, staring ahead of him, out of the window.

'Was fine,' I say.

'Not too hot?'

'Earlier. Earlier it was quite hot. But not later.'

'Ah,' he says, musing. Then: 'David is ...?'

'Fine,' I say. 'He looks fine.'

'Ah. I'm pleased to hear that. I am.'

We look down now at our feet, those interesting objects on the floor. It has become my turn to speak.

'Who ... ?' I begin, but my voice goes out in the darkness like a match.

He clears his throat. 'Gloria,' he says. 'MacIvor. From the school.'

I remember the woman. She is the secretary and has an office next to Stephen's. Though I've seen her no more than a dozen times, she comes vaguely to me now: a plump, floury shape, sticky red hair pinned up behind. A necklace of fake pearls, running across her throat like a zip. Her eyelids are blue.

'Gloria ...' I murmur and, for no reason, laugh.

Stephen is hurt. 'What's funny?'

'Nothing,' I say, and we sit quietly together again.

We have not been this close since our courtship began. Indeed, it is as if we are younger by eleven years and he is visiting me at home, with my mother in the kitchen next door, making supper. I am tempted to stretch out a hand and touch him on the knee.

Instead I stand up. 'What now?' I say, crossing to the window as casually as if we're discussing the housework. The moon is up, and for a moment I entertain the absurd recognition that it's the same moon that appears each day, a lifeless white eye watching our lives.

'I don't know,' he says. 'What now?'

I shrug but I don't turn round. I'd imagined it would be worse than this, somehow. I'd imagined that ten years would make an awful racket and thunder when they finally tore apart. But it's not the case at all. They fall from us gently, those years, slipping off our shoulders like sin and melting into the dark.

'Well,' I say. 'The house. Us.'

He also stands and moves beside me. He puts his arm about me. It rests on my shoulders as a heavy weight. Once again there is a silence; and it seems now that the day has passed like this, in gusts of time in which there is no sound.

'Oh, Stephen,' I say. 'How could ...'

I don't finish. I don't have the energy. This is the closest

I've come to bursting into tears. If I do, I know, I'll fall into his arms and tear at his face with my nails. There'll be no stopping me.

'I don't know,' he says. 'You haven't been here. The house is so empty, you can see. I don't know.'

'Ohh ...'

'We can't seem to agree anymore. On anything. There's a ... a disagreement between us.'

I am listening.

'I need somebody,' he says. 'I can't live alone.'

'I didn't know that,' I say, and it's true. I have always assumed, I suppose, that Stephen could manage quite well without me. I have regarded myself as an intrusion in his life, though perhaps a necessary one.

I take a breath. 'Stephen,' I say. 'Listen to me. This will be over soon.' Echoing his words said over and over, too often, to me. 'And things will be normal again. We'll all come back to our senses. We haven't been ourselves, Stephen, this last while.'

He says nothing. My voice tapers off, becomes a whisper.

'Stephen.'

The moon is inching up the sky. It casts a light into the room in which we stand. I think of her, this Gloria MacIvor, with her pasty skin and her hair dyed red.

Then I stand on tiptoe and kiss Stephen on the cheek, a contact as dry and light as a pressed flower. He doesn't flinch. I go out the door and across the stoep to the grass. My car is round the corner. As I walk towards it, my mother is there, waving her torch like a demented firefly. 'Here,' she hisses. 'Here, here!'

'Mother,' I say. 'How are you feeling?'

'Be careful,' she tells me. She draws me close, holding my

arm. In the shadow of the house we huddle like assassins.

'Him,' she says, pointing back to where Stephen stands, unmoving. 'He's trying to poison you.'

I kiss her too, and go to my car. I start up and drive back round the house, headlights jogging on the bumpy lawn. When I come to the gate I have to get out to open it. I leave it open behind me and set out again on the long drive back to the city.

7

It seems our parting is to be a gentle affair. After this we do not speak on the phone every night. Stephen does call from time to time, but only to ask after David. Linda, I think, guesses what has happened, but doesn't let on. She fusses over me more than ever, plying me with cups of tea and asking if the business at home went well. Yes, I tell her, it all went fine. I leave it at that. But I know even then that I can no longer remain here.

That Friday, shortly before Stephen is due to arrive, I take the plunge. I decide to tell Linda the whole story; there seems no sense in lying. She listens, enthralled, touching at her face now and then with those bloodless nails. When I am done, she begins to cry: a single majestic tear trickles dramatically down her cheek. 'You poor dear,' she says, over and over, her high thin voice scratching like an old record. 'You can't go. You mustn't go. It's he who must go, the bastard ... bastard ...'

Her voice sighs out. It's odd to hear Stephen described that way: a bastard. The name strikes no chords in me. I remove Linda's hand from my arm, I give her a tissue. My bags are packed; time is short; my mind is made up. I thank them both.

I book in that night at a cheap hotel in town. This, the latest in the series of strange rooms to shelter me, is more depressing than any I have seen. It's a dark cell, over-shadowed by a glass-topped wall too close outside. There is a single bed with a brown cover. The carpet is brown. The curtains are brown.

I want to cry, but can't. Tears have become more difficult for me of late, requiring too much effort. But a crack has opened in me somewhere as I sit listlessly on the bed and stare, unseeing, at the smoky square of the television set and the figures moving on it. The crack inside me widens. It's the first night I've spent alone, utterly alone, in my life. There are people who spend fifty years in this way. How do they keep on? How do they survive?

In the morning I phone Stephen at Linda's flat and we agree to meet for coffee nearby. It's been only a week since I saw him last, but I study him as someone long lost. He's getting old; there are lines in his skin. At his temples and in his moustache I discover small silver hairs are growing.

We talk. We agree that David must be told and Stephen undertakes to do so. There are, of course, other matters: a course of action must be decided on. I am all for putting this off, however, till things have eased. I see no reason for haste. It is Stephen who's in a hurry, who wants to talk about moving out of the house.

'But why?' I say. 'Can't it wait?'

'I'm afraid it can't.' He sounds apologetic. 'Gloria, you see, she doesn't want ...'

At the mention of her name, I feel slightly queasy. He speaks of her with warmth, as one who knows her. I rack my brains for an insight to this woman, some clue to her nature or her mind, but can come up only with that vague external picture I first recalled. Flour and dye. I smile tightly and say, 'Of course.'

He tells me he would like to move his things from the house next week. He and Gloria are moving into a flat in town, close to where he used to stay, would you believe it ... He smiles at the thought. I wonder if he ever, when we first met, spoke of me this way. Anger suddenly stabs through me like a knife in the back.

'How can you be so sure you're not making a mistake?'

He looks surprised at my snarl. 'I'm not,' he says seriously, wiping at his moustache with a serviette. 'No one can ever be sure they're not mistaken. That doesn't stop anyone from acting.'

'Oh,' I cry, and the table lurches at my fury. 'You make me so angry, you do. How can you speak this way? This isn't you, you don't think like this …'

'It's Gloria,' he tells me. 'She's opened up another side of me –'

I laugh at him, braying in my anguish. People in the coffee-shop are glancing at us from behind their cups. Unabashed, I go on: 'She has done nothing! If anything has happened to you it's because of me, do you hear? Me!'

He blinks at me, his mouth open. I shake my head, trying to clear it of the sight of him and to jolt my eyes into focus. There is coffee on the surface of the table, spreading in long ungainly fingers towards him. 'There's no need …' he begins, but trails off in exasperation.

He sighs and reaches for another serviette.

I have surprised myself. I had no idea such forces were in me, such jealousy and desperation. But the truth of my words lingers in my head: I am also, yes, I am also proud to have exacted the passion from this man that has been my due for so long.

It is the last meeting I have with Stephen for some time, having stalked from the coffee-shop while he called after me. It takes me many hours to calm down, but, even then, I retain a kind of residual pride in my solitary state, my drab brown room. I visit the hospital only in the afternoon, when Stephen has been and gone. He has, apparently, discussed the matter with David, who seems unaffected by the news.

'Will I still see him?'

'Of course,' I say. 'Over weekends and for holidays. That sort of thing. He isn't going far, you know, just into town.'

'Do you hate him?'

'Of course not,' I say. 'Why should I hate him?' I wonder whether Stephen has explained to David about Gloria MacIvor, with whom he will be living.

'It'll just be us,' says David, 'in the whole big house. You and me.'

'And your grandmother,' I whisper, seeing, as he does, the deserted homestead and we three wandering in it. I try to laugh.

That night I write a letter to Stephen in which I lay out my demands. What has happened, I assert, is entirely his responsibility and, if he wants a divorce, he must obtain it himself. I don't care what grounds he finds, but I have no wish to set foot in court. The house is mine, with everything in it that first belonged to me. I expect money from him each month. I want to keep my car. And David, should he live, is to stay with me.

Should he live. I add this, I confess, with deliberate intent, to remind him of what is actually taking place. We have somehow, both of us, forgotten the tragedy unfolding in our midst. It is now only with rage that I am able to think of the part Stephen has had to play.

It is terrible, I know, but I try to win David over. 'Aren't you sad,' I ask him, 'because he doesn't visit you?'

'He does visit.'

'But when? I'm here every day, in the morning and the afternoon. Doesn't it make you angry that he comes only for a while every two weeks or so?'

He considers. 'No.'

'But you must,' I persist, 'you must want to see him more

than that.'

'No,' he says, plucking at the sheet. He's uneasy; he can sense that I'm driving at something he doesn't understand.

'Does he ever talk to you,' I want to know, 'about me?'

'No.'

'Never? Does he never mention me? I can't believe that.'

'No,' he says.

I become angry at this stubbornness, but I hold my tongue. There is a great deal more I could say to David, there are many matters on which I could take him up. But I know, even as I question him, that I'm being unfair. It's not his fault that any of this has happened.

David, it would seem, is responding to the treatment.

During one of the many sessions I have with Professor Terry at this time, he tells me that there has been significant progress in his recovery. For reasons even the professor can't explain, the extent of the disease has lessened. I understand little of what the professor has to say. All his talk of cell counts is meaningless to me. But there are other signs, small indications of healing that I perceive.

They have removed, for one, the drip from David's arm. The hole in his throat has closed enough for him to eat solid food. And he is allowed to leave the bed. I must teach him to use his feet. An infant once more, he staggers and reels on thin white legs. I hold his arm. But it's not long before he can balance without the support of the wall. We walk each day, up and down the passage. As he grows stronger, we go farther afield. I take him downstairs. We stroll in the garden, a bizarre unsuited pair, leaning on each other as people do in age.

Professor Terry is pleased, but he senses my relief and feels obliged to give warning. 'I don't want you to expect anything,' he says.

'No.'

'I shall keep you informed.'

We are civil with each other. I know he detects in me the resentment I have for him and his colleagues who have, with their needles, torn open our lives.

That next weekend I again make the long trip home. Stephen has indeed removed from the house all that belonged to him. I find myself walking through the rooms, my mother at my side, looking over the furniture, the ornaments, the pictures, checking that nothing I own is missing. It is a strange feeling to be conscious of possessions in this way. As we go, my mother keeps an inventory of her own.

'The small white table,' she says. 'The vase on top ... The picture of the man ... The dresser ... it was terrible,' she says, dropping her voice. 'They came, they looked around, they took what they wanted. If it hadn't been for me, they would've taken everything.'

'Thank you,' I say.

'It's all right, my darling. Sammy helped too. He helped me to stop them.'

I worry for her now, this crazy old woman, but it would seem that Stephen continues to do his duty by her: the kitchen is stocked up. There are dirty plates in the sink. Salome and Moses still come in daily: I have explained to them the new state of things. But still I'm troubled by the thought of the house and its lands under the rule of madness. I explain carefully to the servants that they are not to take orders from her, that they are to see to the smooth running of affairs. 'Soon,' I tell them, 'I will be back.' They stare at me as I speak, watching from beneath their noncommittal eyelids. They do not trade in expression, these two; silent and grim, they go about their business and observe. I wonder if they have seen what I can only imagine: Gloria MacIvor being helped from the car by Stephen, being shown about these now bare rooms over which I once held sway.

As the evening comes on, and the time for my departure with it, I light a fire in the grate and sit with my mother on the floor. The flames colour our faces. This is perhaps the closest and the quietest we have been, she and I, since I was young. Perhaps there have been evenings I can't remember when we sat this way, mother and daughter, while the darkness gathered outside.

'Mother,' I say. 'Are you happy? In your head, are you happy?'

This is something I truly want to know. In the convoluted speculations that are her version of the world, she may find a kind of peace denied to me. But she doesn't understand: she nods to herself and laughs.

I leave her then, after putting out the fire: a sad old woman, unaware of sadness and of age, muttering to herself before an ash-choked grate. Once again I must drive back to the city: a road five hours long, which I am already used to travelling.

(That is our affliction, if you like. There is nothing in the world, nothing at all, which we cannot, in the end, come to accept.)

8

Stephen divorces me a month later in the high court in the city. He comes to the hospital afterwards, where I am reading to David. He stands at the foot of the bed and we all three look questioningly at each other, as if there's something that must be said. But, in the end, it is only formalities we must dispense with: Stephen gives me his set of keys, which open every door to the property at home. He has given the spare ones, he explains, to Mrs de Jager on the neighbouring farm. She will come in each day to look around and check on my mother. He'll still go by when he can, but he lives in town now …

I tell him that I understand.

There are one or two other things, he adds, shifting from foot to foot. I wait expectantly, looking at this tall lean man with bristling black moustache to whom, it appears, I was once married. I see in him, more and more, the side to his nature that Gloria MacIvor has indeed brought out, and wonder if I could have loved him this way. He is less of a headmaster now, and more of a magician; but I have no doubt that, in a month or two, the ink will blot the edges of his hands again, the chalk dust will settle in his hair. When he has grown used to his life once more, he will become the kind of man he was. He may even, who knows, miss me from time to time. But Gloria MacIvor, consigned to facelessness by me, will care for him and cater to his needs. He will have what he has always, in his heart, desired: the little flat in town, bridge parties with friends, and a woman who wears colour in her face.

'You must,' he says, 'come and visit us sometime. I would like to give you my address. If I may.'

I say nothing, which he takes to be consent. He hands me a scrap of paper on which he has already printed, in neat black letters, the name of the place in which he lives. I accept this from him. I put it in my bag.

'I mean it,' he says, as if I have laughed.

'Thank you,' I say gravely.

There then follows another of the silences with which this last exchange began. He sucks at his moustache. He rattles the bottom of the bed and gives, unexpectedly, a smile. 'Goodbye,' he says. 'Big boy.'

'Bye,' says David.

'See you next weekend.'

'Okay.'

I continue to sit, smiling slightly to myself, as if I have a secret to keep, as Stephen leaves. I listen to the retreat of his footsteps on the tiles.

'Do you want to cry?' David asks.

'No.'

'I thought you said you didn't hate him.'

We look at each other, blinking.

On one of the days that follows, as the afternoon draws on, Jason dies in his room at the end of the passage. The sound of screaming is what draws us all; I run from David's room in fright. It's his mother, the woman named Sarah, who asked me so long ago to have tea with her: I catch a glimpse as, thrashing from side to side, two nurses grapple her to the floor. Her mouth is open on a huge and spastic o, giving voice to a cry that we can no longer hear. I back away from her as from a vision of myself. Sightless, dizzy, I push past oncoming bodies till I reach the safety of David's room once more. It's a long time before I have calmed enough to stand again.

But David, he doesn't die.

I reach my decision. On a day like any other – which is, after all, the way he fell ill – I decide he has recovered. I enter his room and stand in the doorway. 'David,' I tell him. 'We're going home.'

He looks at me, intrigued. 'Are we allowed to go?'

'Yes,' I say. 'Of course.'

I realise this is true.

THREE

9

For a long time afterwards, David must be given most special care. He sits out on the back stoep during the day, reading or thinking. He is joined there often by my mother, who perches on the low wall, facing him, and talks. I don't know what it is that they discuss, but she makes David laugh and that is heartening to see.

He has changed, this boy, in deep unreachable ways. He is more of a child than before. He cries without warning or reason. He whines when he wants things. His silliness angers me sometimes and I shout:

'What is the matter with you?' I say. 'Pull yourself together,' I say. 'Be like other children, for God's sake!'

But we know, both of us, that he will never be like other children again.

These thoughts trouble me, but there is much to be seen to. There is the house, for one, to distract me. In the time that I have been away, all has fallen into disrepair. I summon Salome and Moses from their little cluster of huts, where, it seems, they have grown accustomed to spending their days. They are surprised at my return. 'Yes,' I shout. 'It's me! I am back, as I told you I would be!' Stupidly, they stand before me, their faces blank.

I set them to work. Dirt has laid siege to every corner of the house. Insects, too, have taken to living in our cupboards and cracks. There is dusting to be done, and sweeping too. The silver which I used to polish each day has become frosted over and tarnished. Moses, for the first time in his life, is brought into the house to work.

Grumbling and muttering, he scrubs the floors, casting stormy backward glances at me as he does. I don't care. They have neglected their duties, this slothful pair, and it is with vindictive pleasure that I take command again. But there is more to it than this. It is necessary for me to work too. With the hard bristles of brushes, the surfaces of brooms, I hope to erase Stephen's footprints from the floor for ever.

At night, after Salome and Moses have left, retreating into the bush like sullen ghosts, I continue to work, down on hands and knees till my skin is raw. There are blisters on my palms, blood between my fingers, when, late at night, I put out the last lamp and stagger to my bed.

We sleep in our respective rooms now, apart. David appears to have no bad dreams that live in this bedroom of his where, for so many weeks, he tried to die. I, on the other hand, am full of memories about the room to which I must go at night. It is too empty now, too big. There was a chest-of-drawers in here, a table, that have been removed. In the cupboard in which the clothes are kept there are many empty drawers. By these spaces, these absences, do I become aware of the larger absence in my life, and for this reason must go to my bed tired, so that I may fall asleep without delay.

We are done with the house after a week has passed. But if Salome and Moses had thought that their labour was over, it is doubtless with sinking hearts that they watch me go out into the garden. Here there is havoc. Plants grow wild, twining amongst each other like lovers. Weeds are sprouting in the middle of the beds. The edges of the grass, once neatly cropped and clipped, are ragged now as hems in which the threads are torn. But worse than these is the sight of my rose-garden. The ordered rows of tied-up plants have given way to a chaos of scrubby bushes. There are no flowers to be seen. There are only a few petals underfoot, trampled by buck, which have also left their droppings on the ground.

'How dare you?' I scream at Moses. 'How dare you let this happen?'

But he only stares back with expressionless eyes. He cares nothing for me, this sour black man with his hands like steaks. I am nothing to him, a bothersome intrusion in his life that will, eventually, go. The realization disturbs me. I maintain control. *All right*, I think. *I will fire you, then, when this is done.*

But I don't, of course, fire Moses. After two weeks of labour, the garden is restored. By now my anger is dispelled: the sight of the tame green acre about the house is enough to set me at ease. Salome and Moses continue to work, coming in each morning and leaving together at night, as they used to do before the sickness began.

So are we all restored to what we were before. There is routine in our lives to keep us safe. My mother wanders about, watching me from round corners, behind walls. I have bought her a new dog to replace the other that died. This is a frisky beast, also a poodle, that leaps and runs about her feet. I have tied a bell about its neck by which I can tell where it – and so my mother – is hiding.

David, as I say, spends his days on the stoep. He does go for walks, but not very far. He is still too thin and weak to do much, though he gets better by the day. He has missed too much time at school and must repeat his grade next year. But that is several months away, and there is time for healing. He eats well, smiles more. His hair is growing back. I have no doubt that, in a year or two, all trace of the illness will be gone, except for that brown scar on his throat which he wears like a badge.

There has, of course, been trouble over David. I have received a letter from the hospital, signed by Professor Terry, telling me yet again how foolish I have been. The letter I crumpled up and threw away. Not so easy to dismiss was the arrival of Stephen, who came the day after our return. He parked his bakkie behind the house in the usual place (old habits, they say, die hard) and came up to the stoep. I greeted him there, my hair tied back, a wet cloth in hand.

'Yes?' I said, expecting trouble.

'What do you think you are doing?'

'I don't,' I said, 'have to answer to you.'

'Are you trying to kill the boy?'

'Don't speak that way in front of him,' I cried, for David was sitting there, wrapped in a red robe like a judge.

For a long time we glared at each other, this thin long man on whom I had expended a decade of my life, and I. He quivered with rage. I daresay I looked as foolish as he did, with my dirty face, my body wrapped in rags. We had never been further apart than we were then.

At last he left. He muttered as he did, something about taking further steps, but I doubt that he will. He knows too well the replies I could make, the accusations about how he was spending his time while his son was ill.

Such thoughts preoccupy me now. In these familiar rooms, the places that I know, it is easier to visualise what happened while I was far away. This house has been the scene of my undoing. While I sat with David in the hospital, or lay alone in the brown hotel room at night, other people occupied this area. Without my knowledge or consent they performed actions that unpicked the seams of my life. *Where*, I wonder. *When*? I am beset by questions.

One night I cannot bear my bed. I take my pillow and my blanket and creep down the passage to David's room. Blind with sleep, smelling of milk, he fumbles me into his embrace. I slip in beside him and we lie, mother and son, on the narrow mattress. Warm and cramped, I fall asleep.

After this, I sleep here every night. David never mentions it to me, but I sense that he is waiting for me when I come. In the morning, when the first light appears, I roll out of bed and tiptoe away.

I am an early riser. It has always been this way, long before I was married, even, to Stephen. Now, however, there is a meaning in it, as though I must be wakeful as much and as long as I can. It is as though too much has happened while I slept. It is as though I have too little time.

But this is not the case. Now that Stephen is not here to look after, there is too much time, too much time altogether. I find myself looking for means of occupation. There is still a lot to be done, and I continue to clean, to tend the garden. But there are still hours in the day when I am at a loss, when my hands are empty. I try to read, but I am bored, somehow, by words. I play card games with David. I sit in the window and look down the valley.

Every few days I must go into town to shop. I meet people here whom I once knew, who greet me and talk. I dread these conversations for the things they never say. Questions are asked, always, about David: how he is, how he's feeling. He's at home, I tell them, he's feeling fine. But no mention is ever made of Stephen.

It is on one of these shopping expeditions, in the supermarket in town, that I catch sight of Gloria MacIvor. I recognise her at once, though she is not as I recalled: a fat woman, truly fat, with straight red hair cut short. We look at each other down the length of an aisle before she drops her eyes and moves quickly away, pushing her trolley in alarm. I follow. I catch up with her as she tries to make an escape up the next aisle. 'Hello,' I say. 'How are you?'

She keeps on walking. She does not acknowledge my presence at all, but continues to scan the shelves of goods, searching, she would have it appear, for something.

'How is Stephen?' I say.

At this she stops. Her trolley drifts on a little way, bumps into a row of tins. A tin falls, clattering. 'What do you want?' she says.

'To talk.'

'Why? What about?'

'I would have thought,' I say, 'that you and I have things to say to each other.'

'I've got nothing to say to you.'

Her voice is high, as though air escapes through a valve in her neck. She does wear the pearls I imagined: a loose, jiggling white chain at her throat. As she speaks, her face clenches up, then releases. Perhaps she is wrinkling her nose at me. Perhaps I smell bad to her.

'Please,' she says. 'I don't want to make a scene. Just leave me alone. Please.'

'I didn't mean to upset you,' I say. 'I only wanted to talk.'

'Yes,' she says. 'Goodbye.'

I watch as she retreats, leaving her shopping trolley behind. She wears high heels and they make a clicking noise, like an admonishing tongue. *So*, I think. *That is you.*

10

David spends each weekend with his father. It is at these times, while I am left alone in the house, with only my mother for company, that I feel grief most acutely. There is nothing to keep me busy and I find myself pacing the floors and musing. When David returns, I question him.

'What did you do?' I ask.

'Nothing really. We talked. We went to a movie.'

'Did she go too?'

'Yes.'

'Does she ever talk about me? Does she ever ask you about your mother?'

'No,' he says blandly, avoiding my eyes.

If this is true, I resent it. I require her curiosity, as I am curious about her. From what David can tell me, I try to piece together a picture of their lives: Stephen and this woman. David speaks of her, I hear, as Auntie Gloria; and in a strange way she does feel like my sister. She is someone, I feel, I knew well a long time ago.

I am a bitter woman, full of shadows. On the surface I appear to be calm, collected, in absolute control. I run my life decisively. In reality I am full of torment. I contain deeds that have only to be committed. Forces arise in me that I cannot stave off. David comes home one Sunday night wearing a white T-shirt I haven't seen before. A black rage billows up in me that takes me reeling down the passage to the phone. Stephen answers, unsuspecting. Don't, I shout, let your girlfriend buy clothes for my son. Don't let him call her auntie anything, she is the sister of no one in our family.

'Do you understand?' I cry. 'Do you understand?'

Before he can reply, I put down the phone.

By these words, then, spoken in rage, do I come upon the pain in myself.

I phone back later that night and discover myself pleading with this man. 'Please,' I say. 'Please come back to me.'

He is amazed. 'I can't,' he says. 'You have to understand ...'

'Please,' I tell him, believing my words. 'I will die if you don't.'

There is silence, only, on the line.

'Please. Please.'

Knowing his reply, I put down the phone again. I bring my hand up to my mouth and bite into it hard, till blood breaks out.

I meet Cedric soon after this and we become lovers. He is a man unlike Stephen in every way; short, squat, with thick red hair. Indeed, redness is a colour that seems to flicker in him. His skin is covered in reddish freckles. He has ginger hair on his forearms and back. Unlike Stephen, he has no moustache, but a sort of perpetual red stubble covers his chin. He smells faintly of sawdust and sweat, and his voice bursts out of him richly, like oil.

'Life is chaos,' he says, and laughs.

Cedric is a sculptor who lives in a cottage just out of town. I have known him vaguely, on and off, for six years, but never well. With huge red hands, swollen with blood, he hacks out of stone the shapes of animals and men. The garden of his cottage and the workshop behind are full of these strange convulsive figures. They have been excavated, I feel, not from the ground, but from some deeper bedrock in himself that we shall never see. He is an odd man, Cedric, who has never known a woman before me. 'You,' he declares, 'are the first.' Then he releases again that deep shuddering laughter, while I flush in pleasure and in fear.

He laughs a great deal, but finds very little funny. From the first he has moods that change without warning. He is given to fury a lot of the time. Indeed, it is with palpable anger that he sets to work on his blocks of stone. I sit by silently on a little wooden bench and watch as he begins his assault. Holding in his hands a chisel and an iron mallet, he circles the grey column of rock, frowning, sighing, blowing out his cheeks. Then, in a sudden gurgle of air, he darts in close like a swordsman and strikes a ringing blow. Chips fly. Sparks. And from now, without pause or delay, he hammers and pulls at the dark, resolute hunk of rock, knocking off shards and chunks, tearing, I feel, at a dense outer wrapping that conceals some other form beneath. He reveals this, bit by bit, as the hours and the stone go tumbling to the floor. Before my eyes an outline begins to emerge: the convoluted spiral of a horn.

Finally he falls back, sweating and gasping. We are looking at a goat, perched with bunched hooves on an outcrop of earth. Its dark eye regards me from a brute, mute face, animal as the brain it hides.

'For you,' rumbles Cedric.

And laughs to himself.

How is it possible, I wonder, for me to love this man? But I do, I do. This is where I now spend my mornings. In the evenings he comes to the house and eats with us. 'How you doing?' he roars, and pushes playfully at David. Once David falls and hurts himself; he begins to cry. 'Don't be a baby,' Cedric says, pulling him to his feet and dusting him off. 'Nothing's worth tears.' But David continues to cry.

'He's a weak boy,' Cedric tells me later. 'You must be hard on him.'

'Yes,' I say, but think to myself that David has had too much, too much to bear.

'The world,' says Cedric, 'is a hard place.'

He spends some nights with me. We sleep together then in the white double bed in which Stephen and I used to lie. On these nights I do not tiptoe down the passage and creep into bed with David. We do not mention it to each other, this change in our habits, but we are awkward with one another on the mornings that follow.

It is strange to have a lover again after so much time has passed. It has been a long while, measured in nights, since hands have touched me. Cedric makes love as Stephen never did, crouched above me on hands and knees, breathing hard. With Stephen there were rules to be observed, courtesies that should not be broken. Cedric cares nothing for these: we have made love together, more than once, on the cold brick floor of his workshop, with the statues towering about us, and shavings of stone underneath. Though I was bruised afterwards in places on my back, these sore places in my skin were precious to me.

My body (can it be?) has meaning again. As I wait for Cedric in the late afternoons, I undress and bathe myself. I stand before the mirror, confronting in the glass this silvery image of myself, still sliding with soap. My breasts sag tiredly on my chest. There are lines etched into the flesh of my buttocks. But under these, where the body grows old, I see the sites of mystical processes I have somehow learnt to forget. My womb echoes in me, a dark and hollow place. I feel the tides of blood humming under my skin, that each month break and flow. I am warm, wet, mysterious even to myself: a carrier of things. There are seeds in me, events that could take place. I intrigue myself.

Cedric, though, is younger than I, and I wonder sometimes if I'm not repulsive to him. His body is stocky and hard, compressed into a dense red tunnel of flesh. He carries no flab. I am excited by the sight of this man, by the coarse hair on his back and bum, by the rank, hooved smell of him. He is, sometimes, that goat he carved for me: a beast without mind, a driving, biting, savage thing, balanced on the earth.

I think of Stephen, the polite, demure lines of his body. I see him atop Gloria MacIvor and feel, in the slippery pounding of Cedric as he coaxes me closer to my nightly death, a triumph of a sort.

Stephen phones me one day as I am weeding in the garden. For the first time since our parting he sounds unsure of himself. Who, he wants to know, is the man I am with?

I tell him it's not his concern.

He knows, he says. It's only that he's heard from people in town, from David, that I am seeing somebody ... He only thought to ask ...

I tell him again it is none of his business.

Though this is the extent of our discussion, I sing with retribution. Across the miles of telephone cable, I sense the beginnings of his fear.

Cedric knows, of course, about Stephen, but we don't discuss him much. He still exists as a presence in the house and I have kept, for reasons I don't understand, a picture of him above the fireplace. It is a picture taken long ago in which he is bent over, smiling, his teeth gleaming beneath his moustache. His hair is short and neat, cut close to the narrow shape of his head. One night I come into the lounge to find Cedric crouched before the fire, into which he has cast this picture. The frame burns first, curling in the heat. We stand and watch.

'He mustn't be here,' explains Cedric, and grins. The light of the fire is in his teeth.

'Ohh,' I sigh, as if I understand, but the glass of the photograph breaks with a painful, gnashing sound.

After this, it is inevitable that Cedric moves in here. This he does at the start of the following summer. It is a year now since the sickness began, and I take stock of our lives as we carry Cedric's furniture, item by item, into the house. He has given up his cottage down the hill and is to be another person in our midst, a lover and father to us. (I would like him, perhaps, as a husband, but this we have never discussed.) He is also a great deal more: Salome and Moses watch with glum resentment the arrival of their new master. Short and red, loud of voice, he takes command. It is no longer I who control the running of affairs. From the time they arrive in the mornings, the servants are given tasks by Cedric, who has, it seems, a different vision to my own. He sets about rearranging the furniture in the house. This table, he thinks, should be there. The couch is unpleasing where it is. We are all conscripted, servants and family, to move things about. I say nothing as rooms that have been ordered in particular ways since I was young are rearranged in accordance with Cedric's whims. He doesn't like the study as it is; David, he decides, must sleep here instead. And we dutifully move the furniture from David's room into the one at the end of the passage. The study – with its useless arrangement of desk and bookcases – is transplanted to this other space where, night in, night out, David and I endured his illness.

This is not all. The garden, too, Cedric feels, is not acceptable this way. With wheelbarrows, picks and spades, we are required to assist Moses in the moving and removal of flowerbeds. We rip up plants by their soft white roots and toss them down in piles. We smooth over the places where they have stood and cover the sites with grass. Now beds must be dug and we do so, chopping from the even green turf big rings of soil. We lay down compost and plant seeds and David is given the job of watering them each day.

David becomes sullen with the labour. He is unused to work under Stephen's rule and resents, I suppose, obeying orders. But, as Cedric has said, he is a soft child and must learn the way of the world.

My mother, for the first time since she moved there, is forced from her rooms. Cedric requires a place to work, and there is none better than this separate flat behind the house. I try to explain this to my mother, to reason with her, but she wants none of it. She has been deeply disturbed by the sudden frenzy of activity around her. She cannot understand any more than the servants the need for change. She has watched with evident fear from behind her curtain as flowerbeds are erased and new ones created. Now, when I approach her, she bolts her door and pushes a chair against it. I have become strange to her, I suppose, in the way that I seem strange to David and the servants. How can I explain that change is necessary for us, for all of us?

Cedric breaks down her door. There was, he explains afterwards, no other way. In a squeal of bursting wood he invades her room and emerges with her, trembling, into the light. She is given the spare bedroom in the house, to which he has her belongings removed: her ornaments, books, the clothes she never wears. She continues to flutter about her room as Cedric cleans it out, but when it becomes clear that this is no longer her place, she locks herself in her new quarters and does not emerge for days.

So Cedric's workshop is here, at the edge of the lawn. It is from this building that we hear the harsh crash of his chisel. It is a mysterious place, a factory of sorts, to which big chunks of rock are brought, from which those statues emerge. They stand now on my grass, these beasts and men on their pedestals of stone, twisting and rearing all about like images from my mother's dreams. I wander between them in my new and growing garden, looking with dazed confusion on what has taken place while I, it seems, was away.

Stephen phones again. Could we, he wonders, meet in town somewhere. There is something he wants to discuss.

At a plastic outdoor table in the tea-garden in town, in the shade of a dirty yellow umbrella, Stephen confesses his mistake. 'I want to come back to you,' he says. 'I don't know what I thought I was doing.'

I am unmoved. I listen in silence to the pleas of this man, whose skin has drawn tight and tired across his face. There is a patch of dead hair at his fringe. I look over his shoulder as he speaks, at the fat blue pigeons that waddle between the tables. When he is finished, I shake my head. I am happy, I tell him, happier than I ever was with him. He is no match for Cedric. There was a time, I go on, when I would have taken him back, but that is now long gone. Sadly I dab at my lips with my serviette. Then, with infinite politeness and cruelty, I take my leave of him, walking away over the slate path, trying not to cry.

This is my revenge. There is that in me, I must concede, that will not be satisfied by any repayment at all.

'Does your father ever ask about me?' I say to David, when he next returns from a weekend away.

'Yes,' he says, and does not blink.

David is becoming a problem. He no longer talks or laughs of his own accord. He is rude and abrupt with Cedric and even, sometimes, with me. At the supper table he sits, head down, and eats in silence. When asked a question, he mutters as brief a reply as possible and goes on chewing. It is not to be borne. I have stood by him in his time of crisis and deserve more than this. I speak to Cedric about it: the boy must be disciplined.

His father, you see, is soft with him.

Cedric beats David for the first time one night when he is rude to me at supper. He uses the flat of his hand on the back of his legs. The blows are hard and stinging, startling me with their loudness. I go to him in his room afterwards, where he lies sobbing on his bed. It is necessary, I explain, that this takes place. I care for David and want him to be good. David goes on crying, his face in his arm. On the smooth backs of his thighs I see the perfect shape of Cedric's hands, swollen in red.

After this, he beats the boy often. For reasons that begin to seem slight even to me, he will leap up and seize him by the upper arm, whirl him about in the air and lash out with an open, spread-fingered hand. I hear the smack of skin, David's cries. I wonder, dimly, at the process that is taking place. Once, when David on the lawn outside has disturbed Cedric taking a nap, he receives a hiding that knocks him off his feet. I watch from the window as he staggers to the ground and remains there, crouched on hands and knees. Cedric continues to talk to him, using the reasonable even tones that give credit to his status in our house. But afterwards, when Cedric has gone back inside and David has at last stood up, wiping at his face, I see that he has wet himself where he fell.

I go to David outside, but as I approach, his pale white

face seals itself before me like a clam. 'David ...' I begin, but he turns away.

We no longer speak, this boy and I. The equality we had achieved in bedrooms and in hospitals is gone. I see now, for the first time, that he is not as small or gentle as he was. His legs are longer than before. His hair is cut differently, and the bones in his face are changing shape. I try. Another day, another week, while Cedric is in his workshop behind the house, I confront David as he sits in the kitchen. 'What,' I ask, 'has happened to us? Why don't you look at me when we talk?'

'Because,' he says, glaring at his nails.

I must be content with this reason.

Cedric hits me for the first time one morning as he is getting dressed. I can no longer remember exactly what began our argument. I think he bumped his head on the corner of the dresser, and I laughed, unaware that he'd hurt himself. Suddenly I find myself seized by the hair and dragged out of bed. I strike the floor with all the lame weight of ignorance. I am astounded. Still numb, not comprehending, I am raised to my feet and punched in the face. My vision is extinguished, briefly, like the converging light of a television screen put off. When it returns to me, I am sitting on the edge of the bed, holding my bruised jaw, and he is kneeling in front of me, his red face suffused with concern. 'I'm sorry,' he tells me, over and over. 'I don't know what happened.' But I can barely hear him for the creaking noise of my neck.

It happens next perhaps a month after this, in the middle of an ordinary afternoon. This time, the assault is prolonged. There is a malice in it. I have upset him because I was rude with him and, like a child, I must be punished.

He drags me into the bedroom and locks the door. He begins to hit. I back away, I try to plead, but he is stolid, purposeful, to all appearances calm. He advances on me, brandishing his fists like clubs. He kicks me once, twice, on the shins. 'Coward,' I shout, and he twists his hand into my hair, wrenching my head sideways. In all the black-edged panic of my heart, I search for help in the house about. My voice comes out of me, surprising me more than him, a thin, single beam of light or sound: *David*,' I cry. 'Come quickly!'

What he is supposed to do, this twelve-year-old boy with a scar on his throat, I cannot say.

He doesn't come. The door, anyway, is locked. I watch, slow as sand, as that knuckled hand floats gently towards me through the air. It strikes: an impact I register as sensation, not pain. The room shatters, then composes itself again. My one eye is dead, gone blank as black, but Cedric, ever concerned, is propping me up. He keeps me from falling by holding hard to the front of my dress. He strikes again and breaks my nose.

There is a lot of blood. After he has gone, storming out, I suppose, to where he makes form out of stone, I must find a way to stand. I must change into a clean dress without stains. Then, with running eyes, my nose still pouring redly down my chin, I take myself to the car and drive slowly into town.

Dr Bouch, his round lips tight on some deep disapproval, tends to me. He tapes up my nose. He puts ointment on my blackened eye. It will take time, he says, for the swelling to go down. I must be careful.

A silence falls between us. He inches his head forward, onto the pulpy pink cushion of his hands. 'I want to know what happened to you.'

I look at him from my one clear eye. I take a breath. 'David,' I say, 'hit me with a cricket ball.'

There is a pause.

'Are you absolutely sure of that?'

'Yes,' I say, and am surer than I was.

11

It must be said that Cedric doesn't hit me often. Once a month, perhaps, or less, I do something that upsets him enough to strike. But he is always sorry afterwards, when the deed is done. Then he takes me in his arms and cradles me, rocking me from side to side. 'Oh,' he croons. 'How could I do this to you? I'm such an awful person! Awful!'

'No,' I protest. 'It's me, me who's awful! I provoke you,' I tell him, 'into behaving that way.'

We cling to each other like babies and cry.

I take David aside one day. 'I don't want you to tell your father,' I say, 'about what Cedric does. He won't understand.'

David shrugs, looking at his feet.

It's true: Stephen could not possibly understand the passion that must inevitably give rise to violence on occasion. He is, after all, only a headmaster. His hands are soft and slim and have never chopped at stone.

I am given to understand, from what I hear, that Stephen no longer lives with Gloria MacIvor in town. When I ask David about this, he confirms that, yes, Auntie Gloria has moved out. Stephen is alone, in a flat as suitably bare and empty as the home to which I returned. I am sorry for him, I suspect, though am unsure of how.

So it is with dismay that I hear from David that he would like to leave me here and go to live with Stephen. He tells me one evening after supper, while Cedric is in the bath. We are standing on the back stoep, while a bleak twilight settles on the land. David speaks with difficulty and, when he has done, bursts suddenly into tears. For the first time since the sickness he runs at me, throwing his arms around my chest, butting his nose into my arm. He sobs.

Moved, I react. 'Why, David?' I say. 'What is the matter? Is it me? Is it something I have done?'

He makes no reply, only cries.

'I do my best,' I say. 'I try to be all that a mother should be. What more? What more can I do?'

And then, peeved at his relentless crying, the clutch of his bony hands on my back: 'I have sat by you,' I shout, 'to the edge of death! Is this how you repay me? Are you going to that man who did nothing for you, nothing, that I was prepared to do? I slept next to you, I fed you, I talked to you! How dare you leave me now? How dare you?'

At last I pull free of him and stumble away. I stop after three steps and turn back, but he has already gone, running silently and whitely, perhaps for ever, over the grass.

But he does return. There is between us, after this time, a rigid politeness that makes no room for talk. We discuss, when we must, the facts of our lives. There is no further mention of leaving or of Stephen, and I am glad.

'No,' he says.

'David,' I say. 'You will water the garden.'

We stare at each other for a long time. Eventually he turns and, with trembling lip and eyes burning black as sockets in his head, begins to water the garden.

We fight constantly now, as if I expect more of him than is reasonably possible. But small matters are at the centre of our dispute: weeding the lawn, washing the dishes. I set David to work not for my sake, but for his own: Cedric is a hard man and would approve of this. 'Your boy,' he tells me often enough, 'is weak.' To challenge this, to set the record straight, I make David help in the running of the house, taking on jobs that were once the province of the servants, or his mother. But he cannot understand.

'I've got other things to do,' he says. 'I've got homework to do.'

'You will paint your room,' I tell him coldly. 'Do you understand?'

'You're so unfair,' he cries, and goes. But, half an hour later, I pass by his door and catch a glimpse of him on bended knees, holding a paintbrush doused in white paint as in blood. He wields it against the wall. I go in, I kiss him on his head.

'Thank you,' I say. 'I knew I could count on you.'

But he ignores my voice. He does not look at me, only continues to stab at the wall with his brush, the end of his tongue sticking out of his mouth, as Stephen used to do.

He looks a great deal like Stephen, my sullen boy who cannot accept my truce. In the years gone by, since his sickness ended, he has grown a great deal. A small moustache has appeared on his upper lip. He sweats more now, and smells of it. Beneath his skin, his bones have lengthened and grown hard. His voice, when I hear it, is not the voice I used to hear: it's a deep sound now, carrying moods in it, and colour.

'I want to go out camping,' this deep voice says one day. 'For the weekend.'

'Oh, David,' I protest. 'Where? With whom?'

'With friends from school. Just up in the mountains.'

'Oh, David,' I say. 'It's so dangerous there. I don't think so.'

Now, though, he does not argue. He merely stares at me and leaves the room. He has come, I suppose, to expect and accept such refusal from me. For all the work that I would have him do, I still think of him as weak and soft. His body has lain on too many beds, under too many sheets, to lie down on mountains now.

'It's for your own sake,' I tell him later, as he sprawls in his darkened bedroom, staring at the ceiling. 'Do you think I do this for me?'

But he only ignores me as he glares up into the dark.

I do not tell Cedric about the camping trip. He would see it as a good idea, the kind of thing that David should be doing. Instead I show him the other evidence of David's strength: the wall painted white, the garden free of weeds. He nods absently. 'Good,' he says. 'Good work.'

But to David he says nothing. Though they sit beside each other at the table now, and their hands occasionally brush in passing, no word, no glance, is exchanged between them. There is only the soft and monstrous sound of chewing.

There are times, of course, when they do talk to each other, but these are the times when Cedric, with measured, ruminative malevolence, will raise his eyes from his plate and say, his tone pleasant and dangerous: 'What did you do today, my boy?'

'Nothing, really,' David says, fingering his shirt.

'Come on. You couldn't have done nothing.'

And David, his voice and face containing tears, will relate to us all the way he spent his day: the homework he did, the books he read, the trees he climbed. Only when he is done will he bow over his plate and begin to cry hotly into his food. My mother claps gently from her end of the table, an audience of one. I watch, pitying him and angry. And Cedric, his task of kindly cruelty done, will give up his attentive pose and resume eating in silence. After just a few more minutes, he looks up again and says:

'If you want to be a baby, David, go to your room.'

David, soft and edible and pale as the baby he is, must go.

I follow later, to where the light is inevitably off, the curtains, as usual, drawn. I sit on the edge of the bed. I dare to touch him with my hand. 'David,' I plead. 'Why do you cry? It would be all right if only you didn't cry.'

Now, as then, he sobs.

'He loves you,' I go on. 'If you'd just let him, he'd be such a good father to you –'

'I have a father,' David says. 'I don't need another one.'

We sit, while I stroke him with my hand. It's dark in here. Outside, the moon throws down its light about the house, like silver hoops onto a peg.

'Do you think,' I say at last, my voice too soft for me, 'do you think I married Cedric because Stephen went away?'

'You didn't marry him,' says David. 'Did you?'

The question answered, it's too difficult somehow to stroke his back. I let my hand fall and we sit, side by side on the edge of the bed, while the night booms about us in the throats of frogs. After a very long time I get to my feet. Touching at my hair as if it is coming loose, I leave his room.

To bring them closer, I suggest to Cedric that David should call him Father – 'so that you're not a stranger to him.'

Cedric discusses this with David the following evening. Though the door is closed and, after some time, I hear raised voices and the sound of beating, David hereafter refers to this man as Father. 'Here is your supper, Father,' he says.

Or: 'Here is your coffee, Father.'

'Thank you, David,' says Cedric, and smiles.

But David, he does not smile. He gazes back with slightly unfocused eyes, as though thinking about something else of great moment, and turns to leave.

'Where are you going?' Cedric will call from his low, deep chair before the television set.

'To bed, Father.'

'Before you go, come and give your Father a kiss. A bedtime kiss.'

I watch from the crack in the door as David must cross on slipper-swollen feet to the chair, must bend and kiss Cedric on the mouth. 'There,' says Cedric, and pats him on the bum. 'You know I'm as good to you as I can be.'

'Yes,' says David.

'Goodnight.'

'Goodnight,' says David. 'Father.'

Stephen calls me again, angry on the phone. What is this, he wants to know, about David calling Cedric his father? He is no such thing. 'You're not even married to him,' he says.

'Not yet,' I reply coldly, and hold the telephone like a club.

There is a pause. Softer than before, he says: 'Are you going to? Marry him, I mean?'

'I'm free to do exactly as I please,' I say, and put down the phone.

I sit for a long while, hands pressed into my eyes, and weep. But, for all the suffering this would bring to Stephen, I cannot have Cedric as my husband. I think of the long march up the aisle, wrapped about in white. I begin to feel faint.

There is a great deal of silence, now, in the stony house we live in. I speak more to Moses and Salome than to the people who share my roof. My mother, though she seems happy enough in her new room, has taken to wandering far afield each day. She sets out in the mornings, a weird and lonely figure, fading into the bush. In the evening, at sunset, she returns, her wild hair full of burrs, scratches on her hands. I fear that one day she will not come back at all, but I say nothing. I pluck the thorns from her skin and wash her tiny wounds. She does not speak to me. David, as usual, keeps much to himself. And Cedric, fiery, short Cedric who has redeemed me from my solitary state, has lapsed into silence too. He grunts a great deal, though, and scratches his head with thick, gingery fingers. He has brought with him from his cottage a large television set; it stands in the lounge, in front of our now unused fireplace. At night, after supper, it is here that he goes: slouched down in an armchair, eyes fixed unblinkingly on the aquatic movement of the screen. Occasionally, he farts.

I never join him there. I hate the television, and instead I go to my room. So it is at the dinner table in the evenings that we are closest to what I most desire: that small circle of beings, the family. Even my mother is present at these gatherings, hunched over the table like a harmless old predator, spearing at her peas. She munches with an open mouth, surveying us as she does from veiny, yellow eyes.

David hates peas. 'Can I leave these?' he says. 'I've had half.'

'All right,' I say, and smile at him.

Cedric looks up, fixing on David, down the table, his hard crimson stare. 'David,' he says. 'Come here.'

David stands at the head of the table next to Cedric, holding his plate in his hands. It trembles slightly. We, my mother and I, have become quite still as we watch what must, in the end, be a scene.

'Peas are good for you, David,' says Cedric. 'You must eat your peas.'

'I don't like peas,' says David. His voice is very like his plate: a flat, a shiny thing, that trembles on the air.

I watch as Cedric takes his fork. He sticks it into the peas on David's plate and lifts it. There is a pause before David's mouth, as it always does, accepts. He chews.

Cedric feeds to him the plate of peas. Then he reaches for the dish and fills the plate again with the evil green pellets. Again, he takes the fork. David, not moving, not blinking, eats them all. He cries as he stands, but quietly, as if at something he remembers that has nothing to do with us.

Later, as we lie in bed, I say to Cedric, 'That was not necessary.'

Moonlight falls between us on the bed, cold and hard.

'You are too close,' he says. 'The two of you. It's not natural for you to be so close.'

'We're not,' I protest. 'Since you have come, we hardly know each other.'

I hear myself. There are things I realize then, as I lie on the freezing sheets.

'Oh, I love you,' says Cedric. 'I love you so much.'

I don't doubt he does. His fury and his turmoil are his gift to me: the only gift this man can make.

I wander then, for days, with the white concussive understanding of what I have done. Unbeknown to myself, while I was unsuspecting, I have allowed into our lives a terrible force I am not capable of stopping. I stand on the back stoep and look out over the garden, at the new flowerbeds, the statues I do not recognise. I turn and face into the house, in which the rooms, the furniture, have been changed. From far away, drifting to me like smoke, I hear the sound of Cedric in the bathroom. Water splashes and runs as he scrubs, scrubs, to cleanse himself of things too deep for soap.

My mother is beside me on the stoep, leaning on her knobbled wooden walking stick. She giggles to herself, a thin, sawing noise. 'Everything goes,' she says. 'Everything goes.'

'Yes,' I say, hugging myself. 'But what must I do?'

'Ask Sammy,' she says, and laughs again.

'Tell me,' I cry shrilly, 'tell me what to do.'

But she only shakes her head. She shuffles away down the stoep, a frail grey outline in the dusk. She is followed, a little way behind, by the separate translucence of her dog.

Thus it is on an evening like any other, when we have eaten supper and the gas-lamps have all been lit, staving off with their simple yellow light the burden of darkness from outside, that I tell Cedric he must go. We sit in the lounge, he and I, with the television on, but I am in front of the screen. I speak calmly, with the calm of desperation after too many beatings, too many pains, too much sickness altogether.

He listens. I don't remember exactly what it is I say, but they are only words: I love you. I do. But I, we, cannot live this way. It is better to be alone than to have to be this way.

'I'm sorry,' I say.

When I am done, he continues to look at me. The glow of the gas-lamp is in his eyes. He has, it appears, lost interest in me. After a long wait, I leave him there. And it's now, after I've left the room, that he gets to his feet. I hear glass break. Wood cracks. I am back in the room and watching as he begins to destroy what he can see. My mother has left her walking stick on the chair. Armed with this, Cedric is spinning about the room, a man electrified, lashing out in every direction with his length of wood. I see vases break. Tables overturn. He kicks at a bookcase that slowly, uprooted, topples and spills. 'Aahh,' he cries. 'Bitch. Bitch.' The stick comes down.

Strangely, it is in this final act of destruction that I am safest. I stand by, immune, and gaze as he lays waste to what I own. In the end he comes to a halt: head bowed, choking, he tries to breathe. Foam is on his lips. And all about him, spreading, it seems, in ripples from their source, concentric rings of glass and metal and wood move soundlessly outwards.

Later, of course, he comes to me where I lie in bed, wrapped in my nightgown, turned to the wall. He sits on the mattress behind me, a dull and heavy weight. He is crying, loudly so that I can hear. (I too have been crying, but quietly, to myself.) He puts a hand on my back. 'I'm sorry,' he says.

I do not move.

'Please,' he says. 'I will be better than I've been. I promise I'll try. I promise …'

I say nothing. Riven from inside, but still, I lie and breathe.

After he has left, I get out of bed. On bare feet I go down the darkened passage to David's room and open the door. The light is off here too, and I peer into the black. But David, sprawled on his side in sleep, fills the whole mattress; there is no place for me. Aching and somehow ashamed, I close the door again.

The statues are the last to go. After the clothes, the furniture, the books have been packed into boxes and ferried away, load after load, down the hill, it is the statues that they come to fetch. From the unlighted window where I stand to watch, it's a bizarre and soundless sight: men in blue overalls, moving like spectres on the frost-stricken ground, uprooting and bearing away the figures of horses, men, snakes. Cedric watches from the stoep, hands in pockets, quiet. When they come to it, he motions them to leave the statue of the goat. Vigilant and evil, this is for me.

Winter is on us again. Cedric goes back to his cottage at the foot of the hill, where he lived for so long before he met me. We are left again, survivors: my mother, my son, myself. We continue to live, if that is the word, in this house, which has become, though it hardly seems possible, huger and more silent than before. The quietness has overtaken us all, so that our thoughts resound in us like noise. I find myself often standing quite still and hearing, through the long cold passages, the cadence of the jungle about us borne in on the air. It is a slow, inevitable sound: the soft creaking of a dark, immense, relentless progress. All around us, on the hill, trees inch up towards the light. Leaves take shape. Branches, bristling with thorns, are straining for the sky. I mourn.

FOUR

12

Stephen, in the occasional glimpses I catch of him, seems older to my eyes than ever. Though there are no wrinkles in his skin, his face is tired and long. Pouches have begun to form beneath his eyes, beneath his chin. We are all older, I suppose, but it takes a conscious effort to recognise this fact. I pore over my image in the glass, but can see no change. David has grown even taller and has more hair on his body. My mother defies time as she has done since she went mad.

Strangely, it is in Salome and Moses that I confront the passing of the years. I see them one day as the couple they are: grizzled and grey, their dark skins scored and riven like earth. They move stiffly and with pain. They take longer in the evenings, when they set out into the bush, to fade from my sight.

And Moses, it seems, is kinder to Salome. At least he does acknowledge her as they go about their daily business. From time to time I see him cast a glance at her; I see her smile. Once, as they walk back to their hut, the inside of which I have never seen, I see him take her by the hand. Thus joined, stepping angular and awkward as storks, they wander into the gloom of grass and vanish.

So it is not a surprise to be approached one day by this strange black pair, who are whitening as they grow old. They are restless and uneasy, shifting on their feet, as they stand before me where I sit in my familiar window seat that looks down the valley. Moses speaks on their behalf.

Inscrutable to the last, he says that he and his wife are

tired now. They have grown old in the service of this family, having worked for my mother before me. They would like, if it is not too much trouble, if I do not mind ...

'I understand,' I say.

They have a son, they tell me. He and his wife are looking for work, if I thought I needed somebody, perhaps I would consider ...

'Yes,' I say. 'I understand.'

It feels strange to say goodbye to them, this odd twosome who have expended their lifetime on a house and a garden that they do not own. Without warning, as silently as they first appeared in it, they take their leave. Before they go, Salome cups her hands and dips her head in a gesture of acknowledgement; but it feels like mockery to me. Seared, trembling as if I have been burnt, I stand on the back stoep and watch them retreat into the thick green jungle: going, going.

Their son and his wife appear the very next day, like a youthful version of themselves. He is thirty-two, she twenty-five. What they have done till now I cannot find out; he doesn't seem to understand my question. I set them to work like their predecessors and reflect, as I stand back in the shade and watch them, that they too may spend their lives in this way and, one day, take their leave of David when they are old.

This change has no effect on us; we merely go on. My mother, whom I feared would be distraught at the loss of Moses, accepts his son Lucas in his place without a second thought. As if he is his father twenty years ago, she follows him about the lawn and gives him orders.

'There,' she calls. 'Trim there. Hurry it up now.'

David is pleased at their arrival. 'I don't have to work in the garden anymore,' he says.

'No,' I say. 'That's all over now.'

Free now of trivial duties, he spends his time in his room. For some reason he closes the windows and locks his door; I must knock to gain entrance.

'Yes?' he says when he opens, as if he's been disturbed.

'What,' I want to know, 'are you doing in here? Why have you closed the door?'

'That's my business,' he says.

'Don't speak to me that way,' I cry. 'I have a right, a right to know ...'

'Leave me alone,' he shouts, and shuts the door. As I press my weight against it, urgent and in pain, he turns the key against me. I hammer weakly with my fists until, finally, I subside in tears.

This is the way, now, that we must live. He has accommodated in himself a deep, relentless hatred of me that I must try to fight. He speaks little to me. He leaves the room when I come in. His door, at all times, is locked to me, as if I have done some terrible thing for which he must forgive me. Sometimes I crack; with knotted hands I plead: 'What is it?' I cry. 'What have I done? Tell me, so that I can make it better! Please!'

'Nothing,' he says. 'I don't know what you mean.'

'I'm your mother,' I tell him. 'I sat at your bedside when nobody else would. You owe me for that.'

'I owe you nothing,' he says. 'Nothing. Nothing.'

There are moments I suspect this may be true.

To counter his rage, to win him back, I give myself to his service. I prepare his meals, I carry them through to him. I clean his room myself. Often, for no reason, I come to him where he sits at his desk, reading, and hover over him. 'Is there anything you need?' I say. 'Is there anything, my darling, I can get for you?'

He rolls his eyes. 'No,' he says curtly, and turns a page.

'You have only to call –' I tell him.

'Yes,' he says.

With downcast eyes and averted head, he avoids my gaze. At other times, when it is too difficult for me, I sit beside him on the back stoep. He stiffens in his chair, but I speak before he can leave. 'It's a beautiful evening,' I say. 'Isn't it?'

'Hm,' he says, and scratches at his nose.

'I love to sit out here.'

'Hm.'

'What did you do today?'

'Nothing,' he says, and rises to go. He retreats into the house, leaving me to rock gently by myself on the dark back stoep: a silly old woman, smiling vaguely to herself as if at a joke.

There are times when my endless effort angers me. There is a day, for example, when I round on him and, without warning, amazing even myself, I raise my hand and strike. My palm catches him on the cheek and knocks his head around: a savage blow, full of all the other blows I have failed to deliver in my life. He stares at me then, astounded, as he brings his hand up to his cheek.

Later, of course, I must plead with him through his locked and solid door. 'Please,' I say. 'I didn't mean it. I don't know what happened.'

There is silence, only, from within. Beneath my cheek the cool wood presses against me.

For all my remorse, however, there is another day soon afterwards when I lose control again. I fly at him, a woman possessed, raining blows upon his head. 'You are my son,' I scream. 'You must love me, you must …' But my voice trails off as he seizes me by the wrists. Our faces close, straining terribly against each other, he speaks to me through tight-clenched teeth. 'That is the last time you ever do that to me,' he says. 'Do you understand?'

When he does, eventually, let me go, it is I who, with bruised wrists and burning eyes, must run to my room and hide. I lie on my bed for two entire days, hunched on my side, while the pain in my head rages and swells.

After this time, that familiar silence comes between us. We barely speak. It is less difficult this way: he comes and goes as he pleases. When he needs something of me, he asks, and I provide it. For the rest, he fends for himself. He goes out a great deal. He goes, I believe, on his camping trip to the mountains. He has friends, but no girlfriends that I can see. He, like me, loves the forests and goes for long, solitary walks under the trees. I watch him from my window-seat as he goes about his business and remember him as, yes, a little boy who once fell ill.

There are resentments I hold despite myself. I must blame him, I suppose, for what he did to me: the husband that I lost, the lover that I gained. But these were things over which he had no control. I tell myself: *it isn't his fault. There was nothing he could do.*

In any event, it becomes easier now to live with this knowledge. I approach closer each day to my own death, which will make nonsense of my life. I wonder how it is that I will reach my end: will I trip down a staircase and break my neck? Will my car, on one of my numerous drives into town, swerve off the road and smash into a tree? Or will I, old and worn, slip peacefully into death as into sleep?

These are foolish thoughts, for my mother, so much older than I, goes on. She wanders each day on the lawn about the house, surveying her domain from her fierce and shattered face. She comes to me one day and takes me by the hand. Did I know, she whispers, that David is terribly ill?

'No, Mother,' I say. 'That was long ago.'

'No,' she says. 'That was now.'

Time is a meaningless affair to her. She moves without effort between past and present. But it occurs to me that there is a vision in her madness: for yes, the sickness has continued, growing without sound in the combustion of our hearts.

It is shortly after this that David leaves, for ever and for good. He has finished his schooling and has decided, he tells me one day as I am preparing food, that he is going to the city to look for work. He is tired of life out here so far from people. He is tired of the small and dirty town at the bottom of the hill. He wants to go to the big city, where buildings are tall, where things are taking place. A heart is beating, he believes, in the city somewhere.

I say nothing. What is there to say? I smile to myself, because I may otherwise cry, as I slice onions in my hands.

He takes his leave on a still evening soon after Christmas. Summer is at its height. The sun is going down behind the mountains as I come out, and shadows stretch long and pale across the grass. He is waiting on the lawn, a thin, bony figure, the beginnings of a beard on his face. He turns to me as I emerge, as if about to speak. But he says nothing as we face each other in the last blue light. Bats are flickering through the air.

'David,' I say. 'You must take care.'

'Yes,' he says. 'You too.'

'You will come back,' I say, 'and visit me.'

'Yes,' he says. 'I'll write, too.'

I believe he will.

I go to him. We embrace then, on the cooling grass, as

we have been unable to do for years and years. We cling to each other. Then it is done. He pulls away. He bends to his rucksack on the grass, in which he has packed his clothes. He takes it up on his shoulder. 'Goodbye,' he says, and starts to walk away into the forest.

'Goodbye,' I say. I raise a hand.

He fades between the trunks of trees.

I stand for a long while after in the cleared place behind the house. The evening deepens around me like a tide. Above my head the stars are coming out, high, frosty, and far. I am, I suppose, at peace: though the bats continue to flutter about me.

It is a few nights later that my mother starts the fire, but I prefer to think of it, for some reason, as that night: after I turn and walk up from the grass I hear the dog barking and I smell smoke. I begin to run. In my bedroom my mother has set fire to my bed. She stands before it, waving the box of matches in her hands and dancing from foot to foot. 'Burn,' she cries. 'Oh, burn!'

'Mother!' I shout. 'What have you done?'

The garden hose is outside the window and I manage to drag it in and put the fire out, but there is a great deal of smoke. The smell is dreadful. Afterwards I stand and survey the destruction: the charred black square on which I have slept, on which I have conceived a child, on which I have dealt in love. This is the bed, I suppose, on which I too was conceived and born. It hisses now, and smoulders. The wallpaper above it is curling and black. The floor shines with water.

'Oh, Mother,' I say. 'What a mess.'

'Lovely,' she whispers. 'So beautiful.'

She is a wizened woman, too old for her age. I take the matches from her. I see that she has singed her hair; there is a small burn on her hand. Sighing, I lead her from the room. I cannot sleep here and I am tired, too tired, to clean this up tonight.

I take my mother to the bathroom and remove her clothes. For once she is willing to submit to this ordeal. I fill the bath and she climbs in. On the floor on my knees beside her, I wash her. I lather her body, which is a yellow ancient thing, and rub it down. I soap her legs, her belly, the frail shape of her shoulders. I wash her hair. By the time I am done, the water is grey with the dirt of many months. Though I haven't washed myself, I feel cleaner for this labour.

I dry her with a towel. Then I dress her in one of my old white frocks. I put slippers on her feet. I brush out her grey hair about her head and pin it back. Then we both, she and I, look at ourselves in the steamy mirror: side by side at the edge of the bath.

'Time for bed,' she says and claps her hands.

'Yes,' I say. 'It's late.'

'Come on,' she cries. 'No dawdling. It's a long day tomorrow.'

She leads me by the hand up the passage to the lounge. There she has laid a mattress on the floor in front of the fireplace, where the coals are glowing. I undress and roll into bed. She gets down on her knees and kisses me.

'Nighty-night,' she says.

'Mother,' I say. 'Don't go.'

She looks at me a moment and smiles. Over her shoulders I can see the photographs on the wall of all my family gone past. There is a picture there of my father: Sammy, the elusive grinner with his cruel and gentle mouth.

'I'll stay,' says my mother. 'But just for a bit.'

'You mustn't be afraid,' she says, 'of the dark.'

She turns off the lamp. Then she lies down beside me, a thin and parched white figure who is soft, at last, to my touch. We cling to each other. In this way we lie, twined like lovers or enemies, inseparable in our embrace. We sleep.

LOVERS

'No ...' he said.

Then he settled back into the pillows and was gone. Around him the crinkled sheets were like the white surface of a pond on which he was impossibly floating. I stared at him for a long time. He stared back, but his eyes were clouding over, as though smoke had filled the inside of his head.

After a while I stood up. I went to the windows and closed the last little gap in the curtains. Then I pulled the bedclothes straight over him and gently eased his head on the pillow. With the tips of my fingers I smoothed his eyes closed, as they do in films. I stood, looking down at him: a face as white and tight as bandages on his skull. On the coverlet, his right hand was stretched out, frail and grey, amphibian with age. He wore, as he'd always done – day and night, for forty-six years – a gold ring on his middle finger. I touched this ring. It was a cold, hard contact. I bent over and kissed him on the mouth. (I realised I'd never done this before. Even as a little boy on my way to bed, he'd always turned his head slightly so that I kissed him on the tiny dent of flesh at the corner of his mouth.) His lips were cold and clean as the gills of a fish. I straightened and, with a last glance round at this room – so bare, so neat – I turned and went out to my mother.

She sat in the wooden straight-backed chair in the lounge. She always sat here. It was angled towards the white-barred windows and the garden beyond. A pale sunlight came over this garden now, so that the trees stood against it as hard as wire. I approached from behind. I could see at first only her head over the back of the chair, round and dark as a cannonball. (Her hair was actually grey, I knew, but she dyed it black. She bound it up into a dense knot, which she fixed against the back of her head with three silver pins. The position of this knot had never varied from day to day.) I could hear the relentless clicking of her needles before I came round the side of the chair and saw the white wool flickering in her hands.

She was always knitting – jerseys, scarves, socks. But since he'd been put to bed she'd been knitting something I couldn't make out; it didn't seem to be anything useful at all. It poured off the edges of her long needles, metres and metres of white wool, row after row, that now lay collected about her feet in ripples. All day she sat in this chair and knitted. I'd heard her at night too, long after I'd gone to bed. *Clickety-click. Clickety-click.*

I sat in the armchair to the right. From here I could see her in perfect profile as she sat, staring out at the garden. She didn't look down at her hands as they worked. She didn't, at first, turn her head to look at me. She only continued to sit in the straight wooden chair, stately and grim, weaving out like a white web from her bony hands the strange patterns that mounted about her feet.

'Mother,' I said.

After perhaps a minute the needles stopped. She stared straight ahead silently, into the garden, for another moment. Then she did, eventually, turn her head and look at me. I glared back at her. She turned her head to the front again. From her suddenly limp fingers I saw the knitting slide. The needles and their endless strands of wool tumbled from her grasp and fell to the carpet. They made a soft noise as they landed, like a small, perfunctory sigh.

I never saw her knit again.

She didn't cry, my mother – not then, not ever. The days that followed were difficult and sad. I'm not given to tears myself; I have always found them unnecessary. But I cried from time to time over the week that followed his death. At unexpected moments, as I spooned sugar into my tea, or as I closed a certain door, there would flash into me a violent scarlet grief I hadn't experienced before. And I would cry: fierce tears that didn't last long. I tried to remember my father. My earliest recollections were sparse and thin. They were of a tall skinny man with black hair brushed back straight from his forehead. Below his left nostril was a mole, round and neat, with hairs growing from it. Later he would pluck these hairs. And the hairs that made his eyebrows meet in the middle. I would come into the bathroom to brush my teeth before school, and he'd be standing in front of the mirror in his pyjama pants and vest, leaning toward the glass in concentration as he tweezed from the bridge of his nose these small, offensive hairs. He dropped them carefully into the bin. My mother kept a neat bathroom and would have disapproved of even tiny hairs on the floor. We both, he and I, understood this.

He was not fond of words. He didn't speak much and, if he did at all, it was usually to offer advice. 'If I were you,' he'd say, 'I would put my shirt away.' Or: 'I suggest, old man, that you make up your bed.'

My mother approved of shirts put away, of beds made up. She would sweep through the house in her colossal skirts, inspecting the rooms. She made a rushing noise as she moved, like a purging fire.

'Clean up there,' she'd cry in a voice that could only be described as spotless. 'Wash the dishes, James.'

My name is James. I can't help that. It's a name, I

believe, that my mother gave to me. Her father's name was James. She felt obliged to signify due loyalty by naming me after him. Family loyalty is something by which my mother has always placed a lot of store.

Her name is Lydia. My father's name was Ivor. She was born in Cape Town and lived there for the first eighteen years of her life. He was born in Pretoria, but met her in Cape Town when he attended university. He studied business science. He was a businessman all his life, up till four years before his death, when he retired. I knew little of his work. He had an office in town. He would go to work after I had already left for school. His departure in the mornings was an event I could only imagine. I knew his return, however. At five every afternoon he would arrive on the bus. I could see him from my bedroom window, walking with tentative steps up the drive, his briefcase under his left arm. He had three suits, blue, brown and beige. He wore different suits on different days; my mother laid them out on the bed in the mornings. She took them out in a certain sequence, following a private pattern I could never decipher. Perhaps it was the blue suit on Monday, the brown on Tuesday, the beige on Wednesday. Then the sequence would begin again, so that Monday was beige again. Perhaps this was the way it was. I don't know.

I would go to the kitchen when he arrived. I would always go on some pretext, such as to make tea. I would be there as he came through the door. I would look up as he stepped inside, as if surprised. 'Hello, Father,' I'd say.

'Hello, James,' he'd say, and smile. I seem to recall – though I could be mistaken here – that he had a moustache at this time. If so, it has been gone for many years. But I seem to recall a moustache, through which his front tooth, capped in gold, glinted at me.

'How was work?' I said.

'Work was fine. Was fine.' He stood, unsure of himself, as if arriving at a stranger's house for the very first time. 'What did you do today?'

'I did nothing ...'

'You must have done something, James.'

'I did nothing, Father.'

This was true, I think. I did in fact do nothing in the long afternoons when school was finished. I did not have friends. I was not a popular boy. Looking at old photographs of myself, I see a bloodless, anaemic child looking back at me through square glasses. I had a thin neck in which my adam's apple stood out like a knuckle. My hair (the shame of it!) was wet down with grease and combed across the top of my head in an arc. My mother did this to me. I'm sure of it: she would stand me in the bathroom and drag the comb across my scalp like a weapon. She bathed me every night long after I was too old for it, scrubbing my face with the rough edge of a flannel. 'Stand,' she would say. 'Let me soap your legs.'

I hated my mother. I accepted this fact by slow degrees as I grew up, till it resided in me, tiny and dark, a germ that lay too deep for her hands. I hated her with a calm, an easy, and sometimes a pleasant hate. There was no passion in it. She would not have approved of that.

'James,' she said. 'I would appreciate it if you could help with ... with things. It would be too difficult for me.'

'Of course, Mother,' I said. 'Of course I shall help.'

I helped. While she sat in the wooden straight-backed chair in the lounge, I went through his possessions and packed them into boxes. There was little enough to do. In the bedroom there was a small white cupboard and a chest-of-drawers in which all his clothes were kept. (His were separate from hers, at opposite ends of the room.) I had the privilege of touching the garments I could recall him wearing from my days at school. My fingers came into contact with those suits, blue, brown and beige, that he dressed in to go to work. Although different in colour, they had the same fabric: a smooth felt, worn thin at the elbows. I folded them up and packed them into boxes. I folded everything up and put it all away: shoes, shirts, ties, belts. And the more intimate garments that I could only imagine till then – his socks, his underwear. From all the clothes came a faint scent of mothballs and powder. I pressed my nose into the cloth, squeezing it to make it yield up some other odour, some whiff or trace that might give me a hint of a history, an event, a happening in a life gone past. But there was nothing at all.

Mothballs and powder.

I put the boxes into the garage.

'James,' she said. 'If you could help with … with the other room. I would be so grateful.'

'Of course, Mother,' I said. 'I shall be glad to help.'

The other room was the study to which he retired at night after supper. I suppose he worked there, though I cannot guess at what. As a child I'd been in there only seldom, and then only on brief errands for my mother. 'Tell your father he is wanted on the telephone …' I recalled it from then as a cavernous chamber, carpeted in fur and walled in with books.

Now it was a small and modest space with nothing impressive about it. The carpet was thin and pale. There were only three bookcases and the volumes in them were covered in a brown skin of dust. (Nevertheless I looked them over and decided on them for myself.) His desk stood before the window. Light came in from the neat winter garden outside. The walls were covered in faded wallpaper and there were some prints hanging at eye level.

I went through the drawers in the desk. Their contents I also packed into boxes and consigned to the garage. If I'd hoped for a clue here to the heart or mind of the man who fathered me, I was again disappointed. The desk was almost empty, and what there was in it was completely anonymous. Writing pads, pens, staplers, rulers. My hopes lifted when I came upon a tattered brown file in the bottom lefthand drawer, but it contained only some tax forms from years ago. There was not even a signature to be had.

At supper that night, as I faced my mother down the length of the table, I murmured as gently as I could: 'Is there any more to be done?'

She didn't look up from her soup, but continued to stare into the bowl as her hand conveyed the liquid to her mouth in neat sips. She paused for long enough to say, 'No, James. That is all.'

And, two sips later, 'Thank you.'

'It was a pleasure to help,' I said. 'Mother.'

'I thought,' she wheezed, 'that you could have the books in the study. You may have the room,' she said, 'when you come to live here.'

'Thank you.'

'Would you like some more soup, James? It's minestrone and very good for you.'

'Thank you,' I said, 'but I won't.'

'All right then,' she said.

I went back to the study after supper, duster in hand. Sunk into a kind of white and featureless despair, I began to go through the books in the bookcases, wiping them clean, opening them up and riffling through their pages. He'd always loved reading, though she hadn't approved and had insisted after a while that he take books out of the library instead of buying them. 'The expense, Ivor. We cannot afford ...' I also loved reading, and the bedroom of my tiny flat in town was packed with shelves and shelves of books: thrillers, biographies, literature and trash. I tried to imagine now how those books would look in here, in this room: arranged in rows against the one bare wall. I tried to imagine myself behind the desk, my back to the garden, as I sat and listened to the soft slurping noise of my mother's footsteps in the passage outside. It was too much to conceive of.

I'd known, I suppose, that this would be the nature of my dry and tedious fate: to return to this sombre house in which I had been born and spent my first twenty years of life, to become the father I had never begun to recognise or comprehend. I'd known this, I suppose, since he had first taken to his bed on his long, stuttering decline into death. But now that she had made her pact with me, her pagan contract across the shining surface of the table and the steaming bowls of soup, I felt my frightened soul go into revolt. I wanted to scream and cry. I wanted to bang my head against the walls and tear at the drab, fading wallpaper, in which the dim outline of a pattern could still vaguely be seen.

I didn't, of course. I continued to stand, cloth in hand, and wipe stupidly at the covers of the books as I took them one by one from the shelves. In the small oval mirror to the right of the desk I caught a brief glimpse of myself and saw with horror that I was still bloodless and anaemic, that I still looked out at the world through thick glasses. I hadn't even rescued myself from this, the earliest prison I could recall.

At the end of the top row was a copy of *Ivanhoe*. It had

always been his favourite book and I touched it now with a reluctant reverence. As I lifted it down it opened of its own accord in a flurry of dust and gave up its secrets. They fell past my nose, too quick to be seen, and landed on the carpet at my feet. I stood and looked down for a long while before I was brave enough to bend and pick them up.

I sat at the desk. I unfolded the letter. The paper was wrinkled and old and had been rubbed thin with much reading. It was covered in blue ink. The writing wasn't familiar to me; big and loopy and full of sudden strokes and dots. There was a grace in it, and a kind of anger.

Dear Ivor, it said, *I know I promised I wouldn't write, I know you said you wouldn't (couldn't?) write back, but how is it possible for me not to want to speak to you with any voice at all? I thought of phoning you, I have even thought of coming up to Johannesburg to look for you, but I know already that it would be no use. I cannot tell you how I've thought of you since you left ... Only two weeks! How is it possible ...*

Here I looked up. The room before me, with its rigid, implacable lines, wavered and went soft. It was a while before I could breathe properly again and focus my eyes on the page:

... Isn't it strange, the lies that we conceive, the lies that we believe ... What three short days have given us! Or is it only me? Have you forgotten me, wasn't I important after all? Will I ever know? ... I know nothing of you, I know where you live, the room you sleep in ... And her ... You did describe her to me, but she was only more difficult to imagine afterward ... You said that you could never leave her, you said it wasn't possible. I didn't understand, but I couldn't ask. Is it your son that makes it so? Is it him? ...

And:

I remember as we walked out on the last night under the trees, there was a smell, a weight, you could say, of honeysuckle on the air. You said the scent reminded you of things. You said, I think, that it was painful to you ... We searched for the flowers, but we couldn't find them in the dark. After you'd gone I walked out along the path and found the flowers there where we'd stood ... I picked this one, I send it to you as a gift, a token, a remembrance perhaps, but I hope not only that ... Can you smell it still?

I looked past her name – scribbled, huge – to the small dry flower, pressed flat between the pages where it had lain so long. How long? It had no colour, no hue ... I didn't take it in my hand again for fear that it might break, but bent down over it and held my nose close to the crushed petals. Though I strained and strained, I could smell nothing at all.

I couldn't imagine her face. I tried to, of course, over the time that followed, but all I could see in my mind's eye was the sheet of paper rubbed thin by touch and covered in electric squiggles of ink. Was she even alive still? The possibility that she was not, that she may have preceded him, filled me with nauseous fear. I thought only of her, faceless though she was, as I moved about the murky passages of the so-silent house. When I looked at my mother I saw – as he must surely have done – her form moving softly at the edge of my sight. And while we stood about the sides of the grave, suitably subdued as he was lowered beneath the grass, I thought of her in her home beside the sea.

It was a small funeral. He didn't have many friends and, of those, many had moved or passed away. There was the expected group of ex-colleagues and a few sad relatives. I stood beside my mother and she leaned on my arm. I could feel all her frail weight pressing into my palm. As the first spadefuls of earth began to fall on the coffin I turned to glance at her: I saw her stern profile, composed of downward lines, of strokes of flesh attracted by gravity. Her mouth had no colour and, under the tight black hat, her face seemed shaped from some heavy, thick, wet stone. I turned away.

That night at supper she said to me, 'Will you be moving your things this week?'

'Yes,' I said. 'But not immediately. I have to go away,' I told her, 'for a day or two.'

She looked at me; a direct glare full of angry surprise. But I didn't quail. I swallowed a piece of chicken from the end of my fork. She dropped her eyes.

We, neither of us, said more than that. But it was understood between us that I had failed her in a duty. She did not approve.

And I, for now, didn't care. On the following morning, when the sun was high enough to cast shadows in the garden, I left her alone in the dark two-storeyed house and got into my car and set off in pursuit of the address just legibly written in the top righthand corner of the paper that had fallen from my father's copy of *Ivanhoe*.

I parked the car under some low trees at the end of the dust road. Although the house was visible from here, to the right and up, it wasn't possible to drive any further. No other signs of human presence were to be seen; there were no roofs, no cars. There was only the heavy jungle foliage on every side, dark green in colour but static and black in the last light coming in from the sea.

It was dusk; I had driven steadily for many hours with only a single break. As I got out of the car and locked it behind me, I became aware of sharp twinges in the small of my back. (As a child I was always weak. My bones would ache.) The air smelt strongly of salt. I breathed very deeply and looked about me at the leaves that seemed to be oozing from the fat trunks of trees. From over the rise to the right, on the crest of which lights had begun to burn in the house, I could hear the stony throbbing of the sea. It was a sound as relentless and heavy as the beating of my heart.

I wasn't afraid. I can say with certainty that I was strangely calm, as if I knew with complete assurance just what would take place and how.

I doubted nothing. As if I'd been here many times before, I bent under a hanging creeper and started up the narrow path that moved away faintly beneath the trees. The air parted thickly before me and trailed away over my face, slow and warm. After I had travelled only a few metres I could see nothing at all: my car had vanished behind me and the lights of the house were hidden by the slope. The path began to climb. I followed it fairly easily, though I almost fell on roots that lay underfoot like steps. After a minute or two I was breathing heavily and my legs were hurting.

It was a longer walk than it had first appeared to be. As I climbed, I imagined him moving in just this way on such a night as this. So that he was suddenly there with me, exhaling his breath into the warm dark, stepping over the unseen roots, clambering up through the trees towards the top of the rise.

We emerged at last, and stood for a moment to catch our breath. The house was before us, against the edge of the forest which rose behind it in a clean wall. Where we stood, the path petered out into a neat acre of lawn, trimmed and cropped. There were bushes here and there, but no flowerbeds. To the left the ridge fell away sharply again to the beach and there seemed to be another path leading downwards. Standing again under the open sky, it was possible to see the last yellow gleams of sun over the horizon. The sea lay utterly still, utterly calm, like a vast grey field.

She was waiting on the front stoep, a single, slender figure with her arms wrapped about her. She wore a white shawl and a dress of dark wool. The lights were behind her so that she was only an outline. Her shadow stretched across the grass.

I took a breath and started down. I must have come into view only when I reached the edge of the light from inside the house; she gave a small start and hugged her arms tighter about herself. But she said nothing as I crossed the last few metres of grass and came to a stop at the foot of the three low stairs going up to the stoep. I was below her, looking up into her face at last. We stood in this way in silence for a minute.

Then she spoke: 'I'm sorry ...' she said in a faint voice. 'I ...' There was a pause before she could talk properly. 'I thought that you were ... someone else ...'

The light over the sea was gone now. The waters were as black and deep as earth. But another glow marked the thin stretched line of the horizon: the moon, below the curve of the world, was about to rise.

'I am his son,' I said. 'And he is dead.'

She was older than me and younger than my father. I looked at her face in the light of the hanging lamp: her skin was breaking into wrinkles and her hair was beginning to turn white. Her body under the woollen dress seemed stiff when she moved. But she didn't carry herself with pain. She didn't gesture with embarrassment, as some old people do, as if afraid to squander what little motion may be left to them: her hands were big and she used them as she spoke. I had to lean close to hear her voice, though, for it was soft and hesitant – perhaps with grief, or with fear of me, I cannot tell. I don't think she was afraid.

'He was here on business,' she said. 'In town. I met him at the house of a friend. It was a dinner party, he sat next to me at the table. He was uncomfortable, I think, he didn't want to be there. He was biting the end of his thumb.'

'He used to do that,' I said.

'We talked. Rather, I talked at first and he listened. He had a way of listening ...'

'I remember – '

'With his head on one side? I don't know what I spoke about ... Not important things. There were no important things in my life, James ... I don't know if you can understand that ...'

'I can understand.'

'Well. There was something between us immediately, we were both aware that something ... inevitable would take place if we allowed it to ... Can you understand that too?'

'No,' I said. 'But I could, if I tried.'

She smiled. 'I asked him to visit me the next day. Here. I didn't know what he'd say ... He did hesitate, you know ... He looked down at his wedding ring, it was silver, I think ...'

'Gold,' I said.

'But he agreed to come. I woke early the next morning, I waited, I waited ... I was still afraid, you see, that he might change his mind. He was a silent man, your father, he didn't speak. You had to guess his thoughts from other things – the way he looked at you, what his eye fell upon ...'

'I know,' I said. 'I know.'

'He did come, in the end. At noon. I was waiting for him ...'

At this she became quiet and I raised my eyes to the house about us. We sat inside in two cane chairs in front of the fireplace; but there was no fire. The windows and curtains were open to admit the distant noise of the surf. The light in this room – and in all the others – came from lamps which were hung from hooks in the walls and roof. Their glow was yellow and shivery, and fell on bare tiled floors, on simple furniture that was solid and cheap. The house was not very large, but was still too big for what it contained: emptiness quavered around us in rings. Apart from the sound of our voices and the sea, there was only silence here: no noise of engines or children or dogs. It was eerie and sad, and I could not bear to live in it.

'He stayed for three days. He lived with me. At first it was a game – you know the sort of game that people play when there is something that they want from each other, but there are things they cannot tell each other ... It was painful for me, but lovely too, to see him in the house, here ... Not a day goes by without me remembering him standing in a certain place with the light falling on him in a certain way ... This doorway, that stair ...' She became weak and seemed to flatten in her chair like a shadow. She tried to speak but couldn't.

'Still?' I asked, incredulous in spite of myself. 'Surely you cannot *still* ... after all this time.'

'What if I do?' she said, and her voice was hard again. She leaned quickly forward out of her chair. 'He loved me too, you know. He told me so. He said it to me so often that I was tired of hearing it.'

Though I said nothing to her, I reflected that I had never heard him speak those words. For a moment my home and everything in it ballooned in me. I saw my mother as she must surely be sitting, in the wooden straight-backed chair in the lounge, staring out at the garden with her hands folded in her lap. I choked on this image; I tried to vent it from me with speech:

'And?' I said. 'More! Tell me more!'

'We ate together at night. During the day he was out, doing the business he'd come down here to do … He was supposed to be staying in a hotel in town. He'd go back to his room there in the late afternoon to change and to phone home. He phoned home every day, he had to, you see … She expected it of him. It wouldn't have done to arouse her suspicions.'

'No,' I said.

'Then he would come to me, at evening time, the time of day when you arrived … I'd be waiting for him as I was, on the stoep, the lamps all lit …'

'Yes …'

'We walked together every night along the beach. There are some rocks about a kilometre down the sand, he liked to sit there. I don't know why … he liked that place …'

'And you?' I said. 'What did you do while he was out? How did the time pass for you?'

'Slowly. I waited, of course, for him. There were things to occupy my mind …'

'But didn't you work? Wasn't there – '

'I have never worked,' she said shortly. 'I have indulged in … pursuits to busy myself now and then. I have been a painter. I have written stories. But I have not worked.'

'How did you – '

'I was married,' she murmured, almost as if the thought had nothing to do with our conversation, 'once. But he died and left me what he owned.'

'Did you,' I had to know, 'did you love him too?'

She paused and then smiled in the liquid light. 'I did,' she said. 'I suppose I did. Yes … There have been one or two, besides him … before him …' Her smile hadn't faded yet, but bent her lips gently like a taste she couldn't share with me. I knew better than to speak. I waited while she remembered – alone in the bare, cold yellow room, I suppose, purged of my presence for a brief time. I wondered if this was the way she spent her nights; without company or consolation, growing mildly mad in her house on the hill. Then she said, in that same soft tone, 'He is dead now, you say?'

'Yes,' I said. My voice did not emerge properly at first, so I tried again: 'Yes.'

'He's gone then?'

'Yes. Yes.'

There was another pause.

'He left,' she said suddenly, 'after three days. He went away when his business trip was over. I never saw him again. He went back to his wife and to you. He told me about you, you weren't very old then …'

'How old was I? How long ago was this?'

'I don't know … Long ago … Or not so long …'

Her voice trailed away, and she stared at me, clutching a fistful of her dress. Then she spoke, but her voice was harsh now, with a screech in it like wire. 'Why have you come?' she said. 'What do you want from me?'

'I thought that you would want to know,' I said. 'I thought – '

'Why should I want to know? He was nothing to me.' She brought her face closer to mine, so that a drop of spittle hit my forehead as she spoke. 'Did he tell you about me? Did you and your mother hear it all, were you laughing at me all the years and years I ...' She paused, and said with difficulty, 'Were you?'

'No,' I said. My voice was faint now. 'You have my word. We knew nothing at all.'

'How is it then – '

'I found a letter,' I said. 'You wrote a letter.'

There was another pause. She breathed. 'Ah,' she said. 'A letter. Yes.' And fell back into her chair, panting for air as if she had been climbing the steep path up to her house.

I looked at her again, this extraordinary woman whose body had begun to shrink and fade on her in preparation for bringing itself to an end. Even then, when she had sat beside my father at the dinner table however many years before, she could not have been remarkably beautiful. Her face was too round, her chin too large. But I could only imagine what beauty had moved in my father when he'd looked at her. The lies that we conceive, the lies that we believe ... I took her hand in mine. Her skin was as dry and rough as that of a sow.

'You were lovers,' I said. 'Isn't that consolation enough?'

'You don't understand,' she said. 'Your mother – '

'My mother is a wicked woman. She crushed him. He lived no life at all because of her. How he must have thought of you, how he must have loved you all the more because of her.'

'He was with me for three days,' she cried. Her voice was trembling. 'He told me that he loved me more than anything in his life. But she ... she would have known. He said it was no use. He said she was too strong. Three days,' she repeated, and I felt she would have cried if her body was not so dry. 'For three days only, and we were never lovers ...'

'Never?' I whispered through my tiny throat.

'Never.'
By now the moon was up.

The moon was up as we walked beside the sea. It was just clear of the water and, by some trick of refraction or mirage, was huger than it should have been: it hung in the sky like a round, silent, yellow lamp. In its glow we could see the fine debris washed up by the water: tiny shells, sticks, weed, and the transparent bodies of crabs. There were rocks here and there, pushing up out of the sand. To the right the dense wall of vegetation rose in a clear ridge against the sky. If we had turned to look behind us, we might have been able to see the light of her house a little way behind, but before us, other than the swollen moon, there were no lights at all. There was only the dim strip of sand, like a narrow white highway, caught between the land and the sea.

We were walking along the curve of a bay. I could make out, not too far ahead, the jumble of rocks towards which we were headed. She'd pointed them out as we got down to the sand. 'He loved it there.' I was as eager as she to reach this site that had so appealed to him, but even I found it difficult to walk in the heavy sand. Beside me, holding my arm with a hard, sore grasp, she staggered and stumbled in her haste. Her breath streamed out on the still air like the note of a whistle.

'Wouldn't you like to sit?' I said. 'Wouldn't you like a rest?'

'No,' she gasped, and didn't pause. 'When I was young this was an easy, an easy walk to do.'

And on we walked. We didn't talk, partly because we were moving and partly because there truly was no more to say. I felt great pity for the thin pale woman at my side, and even greater pity for my quiet father who had loved her all his life and yet had never had the courage to love her properly. The rocks came closer. And, once again, he was with me there: I saw them in my mind's eye, walking in this way on such a night as this. They were side by side, she clutching to his arm as she was to mine, but for very different reasons. Now and then he would bend his head to hers and they would exchange a few words:

'I love you,' said my poor dead father. 'I wish I could marry you.'

'Do,' said the woman, young and bright. 'Why don't you do it?'

'I can't,' said he. 'You don't understand. There is a force in my life that is stronger than I. I am not brave enough to give up everything for you. She would not, would not let me go. If I had only met you first, before, before ...'

So they walked on towards the cool grey rocks through the dark.

We came upon them almost unexpectedly after such a long haul. I raised my eyes to see them in front of me, close, rising from the sand like a crypt. I came to a stop. She had already halted beside me and was looking with tired and frightened eyes at the luminous mass of stone. There was a smell in the air, such as is given off by water that stands still too long. I breathed through my mouth.

'Is this where – ?' I began, but fell silent when I saw her face.

'Let's sit,' she said. 'Shall we watch the moon?'

She took my hand and led me to a small knoll at the edge of the water. We sat down. She was next to me and had not let go of my hand. I looked out over the ploughed surface of the sea. The moon was high now and had shrunk to a more acceptable size.

She was speaking. 'I remember,' she said, 'when I was a girl, I used to hope for nights like these. I didn't know that they were possible then.'

I listened, but did not reply.

'Is my house too much for you?' she said. 'Is there too much in it? There are people who say it is an overwhelming house. I love the pictures on the walls, the puppets hanging behind the door, the masks in the cupboard, the mess ... If you do not like it, I will throw it all away. Do you hear? If you ever leave me I shall empty my house of everything I do not need.'

Her hand, which had been stroking mine through all this, grew more urgent and insistent in its touch. I could think of little other than this soft, appalling caress.

'I should miss you if you went away,' she said. 'I should miss you more than anything. I miss you now. I miss you when I am with you. Can you understand that?'

At this I tried to protest, but my voice was too thick in my mouth. I grabbed her hand in mine to stop her stroking, but she shook it free as if it had no strength. I could only watch her, lame and dumb, as she continued to launch her appeal:

'Why do you speak so little? You are either too stupid or too wise. I think you are wise, I think you have secrets you know you must not share. You are a silent man. You give no clues. But you have told me that you love me, what bigger secrets can you have? Tell me. I demand to know. Tell me now.' She tugged my hand.

I shook my head. The tide was coming in; a wavelet hissed across the sand and sank away, leaving only bubbles. I shook my head again.

A silence fell. It was cold out here. The air had lost its warmth and a small breeze was coming in off the sea. Also the smell of stagnant water, trapped somewhere in the rocks, was stronger than ever. 'Why do you like it here,' she said, 'Ivor?'

I cleared my throat. 'I don't know. It must be the view.'

'Do you mind if we go back now? I'm tired.'

'No,' I said. 'Let us go back.'

I helped her to her feet. We walked back towards the house in a night that had suddenly grown old. Above the line of the horizon, safe from the bleaching light of the moon, a few scattered stars were burning. I thought of their light, and the distance it had travelled, the time that it had crossed. As we walked without speaking back down the beach, my head was full of visions of her and him and things that had taken place before my life. I saw, once again, my mother as she sat in the wooden straight-backed chair and stared out at the garden.

But that was ridiculous, for it was late and she would have been in bed.

We came to the pathway that led up to her house. I had to help her climb, as she was very tired and the ground was slippery. I wondered how she managed to get up here alone, if she did. She seemed to my eyes far older than when I'd arrived, as if the cells of her body were ageing at terrible speed. Her skin was without colour; it covered her bones like pulp. But I was not repulsed by her. Quite the opposite, in fact: there was in her numb, ancient face a kind of gentleness that made me tender. I touched her with care.

'Thank you,' she said as we came out of the trees and onto the grass below her house. 'You are very kind.'

'No,' I said. 'It is you who are kind.'

We went in. The hanging lamps continued to burn, flickering now and then, but never going out. She lifted one of them from its hook and held it up. The room was

swirling with shadows now, like my mind. I took the lamp
from her.

'Let me do that,' I said.

I led her by the hand. Holding the lamp above, we
moved with slow steps down the long bare corridor, passing
the rooms on either side in which she had expended her life.
They were empty as vaults. As we went, we came to the
other lamps that she had lit and hung before I came. Here I
would stop very briefly, just to put out the flame. They gave
off a scent of sweet oil and smoke. Darkness followed
behind us, lapping through the house. We walked on
without fear, following the trail of yellow light to the room
at the end.

In it there was a mirror and a large white bed. There was
a cupboard. The window had no curtains and gave onto the
forest that grew so close about. I turned away from the
sight of tangled trees, of twisted leaves, to her. She was
waiting for me, hesitant and uncertain. She seemed about to
speak, but her lips were trembling too much.

'Hush,' I said. 'There is nothing to say.'

She nodded at that. But her mouth went on trembling, as
if she were cold.

I kissed that mouth to still its fear, and mine. It felt and
tasted of nothing, like the lips of a ghost. When I raised my
face to look at her, I saw that her eyes were closed, or else
they were blank and cold like the eyes of a fish. I stroked
her hair.

'I love you,' I said.

'Yes,' she said.

'Let me take you to bed.'

'Yes,' she said.

Then I put out the last lamp there was, which I held in
my hand. A faint moonlight came through the window like

water. It cast the shadow of bars across the bed. I took her hand. In the smell of extinguished fire, I undressed her. Her body did not seem old in the blue dark. Only when she moved, as she did when I helped her onto the bed, could I hear the age of her creaking bones and painful sighs. She lay and waited for me.

She didn't wait long. But I did pause a moment to think before I performed this final act – perhaps the only act of kindness allowed me in my life. But it was more than that. There was a kind of love in it, and a passion too. It gave her peace, and him. Perhaps it also gave me peace. I cannot say for sure.

Afterwards, as she lay sleeping, I dressed beside the bed. I looked at her one final time. Then I left the room, closing the door behind me. I walked back through the darkened house, passing the lamps that hung like steel fruit from the ceiling. The front door was open and I went through, out onto the cold grass. I stood there for a minute, just to tuck in my shirt and to look for the moon which had already gone. The sky in the east was beginning to go pale, for the world had turned once and the sun had returned. I walked across the grass, leaving footprints in the dew. I reached the path and started down to my car.

I stopped only once on the way down. There was a smell, a weight, you could say, of honeysuckle on the air. It lasted only a moment and I could have been mistaken. I pressed on.

SHADOWS

The two of us are pedalling down the road. The light of the moon makes shadows under the trees, through which we pass, going fast. Robert is a little ahead of me, standing up in his seat. On either side of his bike the dogs are running, Ben and Sheba, I can never tell the difference between them.

It's lovely to be like this; him and me, with the warm air going over us like hands.

'Oh,' I say. 'Oh, oh, oh ...'

He turns, looking at me over his shoulder. 'What?' he calls.

I shake my head at him. He turns away.

As we ride, I can see the round shape of the moon as it appears between the trees. With the angle of the road it's off to the right, above the line of the slope. The sky around it is pale, as if it's been scrubbed too long. It hurts to look up.

It's that moon we're riding out to see. For two weeks now people have talked about nothing else. 'The eclipse,' they say. 'Are you going to watch the eclipse?' I didn't understand at first, but my father explained it to me. 'The shadow of the earth,' he says, 'thrown across the moon.' It's awesome to think of that, of the size of some shadows. When people ask me after this, I tell them, 'Yes,' I tell them. 'I'm going to watch the eclipse.'

But this is Robert's idea. A week ago he said to me, 'D'you want to go down to the lake on Saturday night? We can watch the eclipse from there.'

'Yes,' I said. 'We can do that.'

So we ride down towards the lake under the moon. On

either side the dogs are running, making no sound in the heavy dust, their tongues trailing wetly from the corners of their mouths.

The road is beginning to slope down now as we come near to the lake. The ground on either side becomes higher, so that we're cycling down between two shoulders of land. The forest is on either side, not moving in the quiet air. It gives off a smell: thick and green. I breathe deeply, and my lungs are full of the raw, hairy scent of the jungle.

We're moving quite fast on the downhill, so we don't have to pedal anymore. Ahead of me, I see Robert break from the cut in the road and emerge again into the flat path that runs across the floor of the forest. A moment later I do so too, whizzing into the heavy layers of shadows as if they are solid. The momentum is wonderful, full of danger, as if we're close to breaking free of gravity. But it only lasts a moment. Then we're slowing again, dragged back by the even surface of the road and the sand on the wheels.

The turnoff is here. I catch up with Robert and we turn off side by side, pedalling again to keep moving. Ahead of us the surface of the lake is between the trees, stretched out greenly in the dark. The trees thin out, there's a bare strip along the edge of the water.

We stop here. The path we were riding on goes, straight and even, into the water. That's because it used to lead somewhere before they flooded the valley to make the lake. They say that under the water there are houses and gardens, standing empty and silent in the currents below. I think of them and shiver. It's always night down there at the bottom of the lake; the moon never shines.

But we've stopped far from where the path disappears. We're still side by side, straddling the bikes, looking out. The dogs have also stopped, stock-still, as if they can smell something in the air. There's a faint wind coming in off the water, more of a breeze really. On the far side of the lake we can see the lights of houses. Far off to the right, at the furthest corner of the water, are the lights of my house. I glance towards it and try to imagine them: my father and mother, sitting out on the front veranda, looking across the water to us. But there are no lights where we are.

'There,' says Robert.

He's pointing. I follow his finger and I also see it: the moon, clear of the trees on the other side. It really is huge tonight, as if it's been swollen with water. If you stare at it for long enough you can make out the craters on its surface, faint and blue, like shadows. Its light comes down softly like rain and I see I was wrong – it makes the water silver, not green.

'We've got a view of it,' I say.

But Robert is moving away already. 'Come,' he says. 'Let's make a fire.'

We leave the bikes leaning together against the trunk of a tree and set out to look for firewood. We separate and walk out by ourselves into the forest. But I can still see Robert a little distance away as he wanders around, bending now and then to pick up bits of wood. The dogs are with him. It isn't dense or overgrown down here. The floor of the forest is smooth. Apart from the sound of our feet and the lapping of the lake, it's quiet here.

There isn't much dead wood around. I pick up a few branches, some chunks of log. I carry them down to where the bikes are. Robert has already made one trip here, I see from a small pile of twigs. I don't much feel like this hunting in the dark, so I delay a while, wiping my hands on my pants. I look out over the water again. I feel so calm and happy as I stand, as if the rest of my life will be made up of evenings like this. I hear Robert's whistling coming down to me out of the dark behind. It's a tune I almost recognise. I start to hum along.

As I do I can see Robert in my mind's eye, the way he must be. When he whistles, small creases appear round his lips. He has a look of severe concentration on his face. The image of him comes often to me in this way, even when I'm alone. Sometimes late at night as I lie trying to sleep, a shadow cast in from outside will move against the wall and then he breaks through me in a pang, quick and deep. We've been friends for years now, since I started high school. It's often as if I have no other friends. *He* has, though. I see him sometimes with other boys from the school, riding past my house in a swirling khaki pack down to the lake. It hurts me when this happens. I don't know what they speak about, whether they talk of things that I could understand. I wonder sometimes if they mention me. I wonder if they mock me when I'm not there and if Robert laughs at me with the rest of them.

He comes down now, carrying a load of wood in his arms. 'Is that all?' he says, looking at what I collected. 'What's the matter with you?'

'Nothing,' I say, and smile.

He drops his wood along with the rest and turns. He's grinning at me: a big skew grin, little bits of bark stuck to his hair and the front of his shirt.

'Do we need any more?'

'No,' he says. 'That should do fine.'

We build a fire. Rather – he builds the fire and I sit against a tree to watch. It always seems to be this way: him doing the work, me watching. But it's a comfortable arrangement, he doesn't mind. I like the way he moves. He's a skinny boy, Robert, his clothes are always slightly loose on him. Now as I watch, my eye is on his hands as they reach for the wood and stack it. His hands are slender and brown. He's brought a wad of newspaper on his bike. He twists rolls of paper into the openings between the logs.

Like me, the dogs are sitting still and watching. They stare at him with quiet attention, obedient and dumb.

He lights the fire. He holds the burning match and I'm looking for a moment at this white-haired boy with flame in his hand. Then he leans and touches it to the paper. Smoke. He shakes out the match.

The fire burns, the flames go up. In a minute or two there's a nice blaze going. We're making our own light to send across the water. I think of my parents on the wooden veranda, looking across to the spark that's started up in the darkness. They point. 'There,' they say. 'That's where they are.' I smile. The fire burns. The flames go up. The heat wraps over my face like a second skin. The dogs get up and move away, back into the dark where they shift restlessly, mewing like kittens.

In a little time the fire burns down to a heap of coals. They glow and pulse, sending up tiny spurts of flame. We only have to throw on a stick now and then. Sitting and staring into the ring of heat, it would be easy to be quiet, but we talk, though our voices are soft.

'We should camp out here sometime,' he says. 'It's so still.'

'Yes,' I say. 'We should do that.'

'It's great to be away,' he says. 'From them.'

He's speaking of his family; his home. He often speaks of them this way. I don't know what he means by this: they all seem nice enough. They live in a huge, two-storeyed house made out of wood, about half an hour's ride from us. They're further up the valley, though, out of sight of the lake. There are five of them: Robert, his parents, his two brothers. I'm alone in my home, I have no brothers. Perhaps it's this that makes their house a beautiful place to me. Perhaps there really is something ugly in it that I haven't seen. Either way, we don't spend much time there. It's to my home that Robert likes to come in the afternoons when school is done. He's familiar to us all. He comes straight up to my room, I know the way he knocks on my door. Bang--bang, thud.

My mother has spoken to me about him. At least twice that I can remember she's sat on my bed, smiling at me and playing with her hands.

'But what's wrong with it?' I say. 'Everyone has friends.'

'But lots,' she says. 'Lots of friends. You do nothing else, you see no one else ...'

'There's nothing else to do,' I say. 'Other people bore me.'

'There's sport,' she says. 'I've seen them at the school, every afternoon. Why don't you play sport like other boys? You're becoming thinner and thinner.'

It's true. I am. When I look at myself in the mirror I'm surprised at how thin I am. But I'm not unhealthy, my skin is dark, I'm fit. We ride for miles together, Robert and me, along the dust roads that go around the lake.

'It's him,' I say. 'Isn't it? It's him you don't like.'

'No,' she says. 'It isn't that. I like him well enough. It's you, you that's the matter.'

I don't want to upset them, my parents. I want to be a good son to them. But I don't know any way to be fatter than I am, to please them. I do my best.

'I'll try,' I say. 'I'll try to see less of him.'

But it doesn't help. Most afternoons I hear his knock at my door and I'm glad at the sound. We go out on our bikes.

This happens at night too, from time to time. As now – when we find ourselves at the edge of the lake, staring at the moon.

'D'you want a smoke?' he says.

I don't answer. But he takes one out of the box anyway, leaning forward to light it in the fire. He puffs. Then he hands it to me. I take a drag, trying to be casual. But I've never felt as easy about it as Robert seems to. The smoke is rough in my throat, it makes my tongue go sour. I don't enjoy it. But for the sake of Robert I allow this exchange to take place, this wordless passing back and forth, this puffing in the dark. I touch his hand as I give it back to him.

'Are you bored?' he asks. 'Why're you so quiet?'

'No,' I say. 'I'm fine.' I think for a while, then ask, 'Are you?'

'No,' he says.

But I wonder if he is. In sudden alarm I think of the places he might rather be, the people he might rather be with. To confirm my fear, he mutters just then:

'Emma Brown – '

'Why are you thinking about Emma Brown?' I say. 'What made you think of her now?'

He's looking at me, surprised. He takes the cigarette out of his mouth. 'I was just wondering,' he says. 'I was just wondering where she is.'

'Why?' I say.

'I just wondered if she was also watching the moon.'

'Oh,' I say, and smile bitterly into the fire. I don't know what's going through his head, but mine is full of thoughts of her: of silly little Emma Brown, just a bit plump, with her brown hair and short white socks. I remember a few times lately that I've seen her talking to Robert; I remember him smiling at her as she came late to class.

'I was just thinking,' he says, and shrugs.

I finish the cigarette. I throw the butt into the fire. We don't talk for a long time after that. I can hear the dogs licking each other, the rasping noise of their tongues. I begin to feel sad. I think of my anger and something in me slides, as if my heart is displaced.

He reaches out a hand and grazes my arm. It's just a brief touch, a tingle of fingers, but it goes into me like a coal. 'Hey,' he says. 'What's the matter?'

'Nothing,' I say. 'Nothing.' I want to say more, but I don't like to lie. Instead I say again, 'Nothing.' I feel stupid.

The fire burns down to a red smear on the ground. Across the water the lights have started to go out. Only a few are left. I look off to the right: the lights in my house are still on. My parents keep watch.

When I look back, Robert is on his feet. His head is thrown back. I don't stand, but I gaze over his shoulder at what he's watching: the white disc of the moon, from which a piece has been broken. While we were talking, the great shadow of the earth has started to cover the moon. If you look hard enough, the dark piece can still be seen, but only in outline, as if it's been sketched with chalk.

We stare for a long time. As we do, the shadow creeps on perceptibly. You can actually see it move.

'Wow,' he says.

Sensing something, one of the dogs throws back its head in imitation of us and begins to howl. The noise goes up, wobbling on the air like smoke.

'Sheba,' says Robert. 'Be quiet.'

We watch the moon as it sinks slowly out of sight. Its light is still coming down, but more faintly than before. On the whole valley, lit weirdly in the strange blue glow, a kind of quiet has fallen. There is nothing to say. I lower my eyes and look out over the water. Robert sits down next to me on his heels, hugging his knees. 'You know,' he says, 'there's times when everything feels … feels …'

He doesn't finish.

'I know,' I say.

We sit and watch. Time goes by. The trees are behind us, black and big. I look across to my home again and see that the lights have gone out. All along the far shore there is dark. We're alone.

'It's taking a long time,' he says. 'Don't you think?'

'Yes,' I say. 'It is.'

It's hot. The dogs are panting like cattle in the gloom. I feel him along my arm. A warmth. I spring up, away. 'I'm going to swim,' I say, unbuttoning my shirt.

I take off my clothes, and drop them on the sand. The dogs are standing, staring at me. Robert also watches, still crouched on his heels, biting his arm. When I'm naked I turn my back on him and walk into the lake. I stop when the water reaches my knees and stand, arms folded across my chest, hands clinging to my ribs as if they don't belong to me. It isn't cold, but my skin goes tight as if it is. One of the dogs lets out a bark. I walk on, hands at my sides now, while the water gets higher and higher. When it reaches my hips I dive. It covers my head like a blanket. I come up, spluttering. 'It's warm,' I say, 'as blood.'

'Hold on,' he calls. 'I'm –'

As I turn he's already running. I catch a glimpse of his body, long and bright as a blade, before he also dives. When he comes up, next to me, the air is suddenly full of noise: the barking of the dogs as they run along the edge of the lake, the splashing of water, the shouts of our voices. It is our voices I hear, I'm surprised at the sound. I'm laughing. I'm calling out.

'Don't you,' I say, 'don't you *try –*'

We're pushing at each other, and pulling. Water flies. The bottom of the lake is slippery to my feet, I feel stones turn. I have hold of Robert's shoulder. I have a hand in his hair. I'm trying to push him under, wrenching at him while he does the same to me. He laughs.

Nothing like this has taken place between us before. I feel his skin against me, I feel the shape of his bones as we wrestle and lunge. We're touching each other. Then I slide, the water hits my face. I go under, pulling him with me, and for a moment we're tangled below the surface, leg to leg, neck to neck, furry with bubbles, as if we'll never pull free.

We come up together into quiet. The laughter has been doused. We still clutch to each other, but his fingers are hurting me. We stand, face to face. While we were below, the last sliver of moon has been blotted out. A total dark has fallen on the valley, so that the trees are invisible against the sky. The moon is a faint red outline overhead. I can't see Robert's face, though I can feel his breath against my nose. We gasp for air. The only sound to be heard is the howling of the dogs that drifts in from the shore: an awful noise, bereaved and bestial.

I let go. And he lets go of me. Finger by finger, joint by joint, we release one another till we are standing, separate and safe, apart. I rub my arm where he hurt it.

'Sorry,' he mutters.

'It's okay,' I say. 'It doesn't matter.'

After that we make our way to shore. I wade with heavy steps, as if through sand. By the time I reach the edge and am standing, dripping, beside my clothes, the moon has begun to emerge from shadow and a little light is falling. The dogs stop howling. I don't look up as I dress. I put my clothes on just so, over my wet body. They stick to me like mud.

I wait for him to finish dressing. As he ties his shoelaces I say, not even looking at him, 'What d'you think will happen?'

'What d'you mean?' he says.

'To us,' I say. 'D'you think in ten years from now we're even going to know each other?'

'I don't know what you mean,' he says.

He sounds irritated as he says this, as if I say a lot of things he doesn't understand. Maybe I do. I turn away and start to walk back to the bikes.

'Hey,' he calls. 'What you … don'tcha want another smoke or somethin' before we go?'

'No,' I say. 'Not me.'

I wait for him at the tree where the bikes are leaning. He takes his time. I watch him scoop water over the coals. They make a hissing noise, like an engine beneath the ground. Then he walks up towards me along the bank, hands in his pockets. The sight of him this way, sulking and slow, rings in me long after we've mounted our bikes and started back up the path.

By the time we rejoin the dust road a little way on, the soreness in me is smaller than it was. One of the dogs runs into his way and he swears. At this I even manage to laugh. I look off and up to the left, at the moon which is becoming rounder by the minute. Its light comes down in soft white flakes, settling on us coldly as we ride.

THE CLAY OX

I stood at the roadside for perhaps half an hour before she stopped for me. I looked around. Countless cars went past. There were pebbles next to my boots. Yellow grasslands shimmered away on either side. I turned my head once and spat – a little star of gob that began to sizzle gently on the tar.

Then she pulled up. She drove a white Volkswagen beetle. There was a rubber skeleton dangling from the mirror.

'Where to?' she said.

'Where are you going?' I opened the door before she could answer. I didn't actually know where I was, what road precisely I had stood beside for a forty-eighth part of a day. Harrismith was the last town I'd seen. I didn't know in what direction it now lay. I slid in beside her and closed the door. The window was open, so I rested my arm along it. I stared straight in front of me.

'Hey,' she said. Her voice was furry, the words lifted from her lips like soap-bubbles. I must confess I liked it immediately. 'Hey,' she said. 'You must be going *somewhere*.'

'Aren't we all?' I said. Ever the cynic. I suspect she smiled then, I can't say for sure; I wasn't looking at her. But it was then that she put the car in gear and swung out onto the road. As we gathered speed, warm corrugations of air pushed against my face. On either side of us the landscape spread like a silent yellow foam. I put on my seat-belt.

Much later she confided that she'd been afraid of me. A

little, anyway. My browns were filthy, stiff with dew and sap and other excretions that I'd collected nightly in roadside hollows. It seemed that I was doomed to inhabit the edges of roads until I reached the end of mine. I stank. My hair was unbrushed. Bristles covered my chin. The skin of my hands had been broken by thorns. But it didn't occur to me that I may have been frightening to look at. Perhaps it was just that I didn't care much for the feelings of others after a thousand kilometres of desert and veld.

'I thought soldiers were supposed to be neat,' she said after we'd driven for five minutes in silence. Then: 'Aren't they?' when it became clear I wasn't going to agree.

'I'm not a soldier,' I said shortly and looked out of the window.

'No?' She glanced at my bedraggled uniform and discoloured boots. Then she leaned forward and pressed a tape into the deck below the dashboard. Beethoven. The Moonlight Sonata. Even in the interior of the Volkswagen those moth-soft notes were perfect enough to be painful. I smiled, not quite at her.

'You like?'

I nodded and looked in front of me again. In the swift sideways turn of my head I'd caught a peripheral glimpse of white-blonde hair cut raggedly short.

'What's your name?' she said.

'Guy.'

'Don't you look people in the face, Guy?'

'No.'

Before us the road ran grey. Hillocks heaved up from the plain here, like mounds covering the mass graves of men killed in fighting.

'Don't you want to know *my* name, Guy?' she asked.

'No.'

'You're weird, aren't you?'

So I looked her in the face. I think it was the first face I'd met with my eyes in more than a month. She smiled at me. Her teeth were uneven. She wore no makeup and the angles of her cheeks and jaw trapped small smears of shadow in her skin. I smiled thinly back at her.

'Where are you going?' The second time I'd asked.

'I'm going to the mountains,' she said. 'To the Drakensberg for a day or two.'

It was agreed between us, though not with words, that I would accompany her. I turned away and looked out of my window again.

As a child I had lived among green hills and like a hummingbird had craved the sweat of flowers. At night I walked through plantations where leaves fell quiet as scent across the white moon. Now I carried behind my forehead the discord of barbed wire, of boot-battered parade grounds, of human eyes like those of dogs flickering redly from the dark. Flight had promised to accelerate my descent towards the thrilling detonation of my own extinction. Having begun, one cannot stop. Foot before foot, wrenching the prison of the tattered soul endlessly forward, one staggers across deserts to get away.

If I had been asked, I would have said that I was raised in Tzaneen and that I had been a boarder at Pretoria Boys' High School. I was an anonymous boy, one among many. I would have admitted that my parents were divorced and, if pressed, that my mother had remarried. But that would have been the limit of any confession on my part. To say any more would be against the values taught me by my father, who is a good man. He allows me to call him by his first name. He is Geoff. Geoff fought in the Second World

War and carries a distinctive scar on his back.

Before he left there were many pleasurable evenings when Geoff would play his records. We would sit on the outside stoep and listen. The sweetest voice I'd ever heard came to me through the open windows and through some more secret opening in the four decades that prised us apart. Geoff told me her name was Vera Lynn. Vera sang to us on those evenings such delicious vows as 'I know we'll meet again some sunny day'. I trusted Vera. I believed her. 'There'll be peace and laughter,' she sang, 'forever after, tomorrow, when we are free.'

My stepfather is not like Geoff at all. I know from the start that stepfathers are by tradition formidable and cruel and so I try to accommodate this man by saying it is difficult for him and I must be patient. In reality he is formidable and cruel. He is short and squat with reddish hair. His lips are like pink slugs. Also, I can't understand him. He speaks Afrikaans and he speaks it very quickly. His arms are long and his hands are hard. He strikes me often with his fist against my head.

On a certain day, for reasons too complex for me to comprehend, he locks my mother in her room. He stands outside the door and listens to her cries. By now I have run and am sitting on my bed, shaking. I can feel violence colouring the air. I have seen it growing like this before. My stepfather tolerates nothing and lashes out with his hard fists on their long arms. He has knocked down our black gardener when he becomes impertinent. I have heard him break my mother's nose and blacken her eyes. And, as I have said, he strikes me often with his fist against my head. I am terribly afraid of him.

'If you don't let me out,' my mother says, 'I'll break the window.'

He does not reply. But I sense him standing darkly at her door, folding up his thick red fingers into a fist.

'One, two, three,' my mother cries.

I hear glass break. Hanging out of my window, I see her lunging with a wooden walking stick. The noise is jagged and harsh. It goes on until she has knocked every last fragment from the frame. The shards lie jumbled and sharp among the brilliant blooms that blaze like fire outside their room.

Now my stepfather twists the little stub of metal in the lock and swings open the door. 'Take your son and get out,' he says.

This is a violence of a different kind. Weeping, my mother stumbles with me to the car. I sit in the back seat, unable to comprehend why she is not as joyful as I am to be leaving. She doesn't start the engine. 'Wait here,' she says and goes back inside. I am afraid for her, but I do as I am told. I wait. I wait. After an hour has passed I get out and go inside, expecting death. The house is quiet. I tiptoe to my mother's room. Through the crack in the door I see them both, side by side on the bed. Their hands are joined. Cold winds blow in through the broken window, passing over and between them as they lie sleeping.

My first impression of those mountains was not overwhelming. Dusk was already falling as we approached along abominable dust roads, following obscure signposts on either side. I'd never been to the Drakensberg before, though I'd heard of them. They were a part of our history. The Boers, I knew, had crossed them on their trek into the interior. I looked forward to seeing them, I was ready to be impressed. But there was nothing to see. After a while I gave up straining my eyes.

Far more arresting on either side was the presence of a million tiny hovels, built from tin and mud and broken stones. There did truly seem to be millions of them, going on and on as far as the eye could see. I could make out patterns on the walls. The torn roofs and windows suggested that this ugly city was in fact a ruin. I was prepared to accept, with relief, that people didn't live here. But there were fires, enormous, ghostlike and soundless, inside these buildings. The red light from the flames sketched on the twilight the outlines of doorways and openings. 'My God,' I said. 'Who lives here?'

As I spoke, two figures came into the yellow beam of the headlamps. She braked and the car slid across the thick dust surface of the road. The instant we came to a halt the figures were at either window, craning in, holding objects of dried clay in their dust-reddened hands. I saw only figures reaching for me, savage motion blurred by dark. I was afraid. I cried:

'What is it? What do they want?'

Their jabbering was shrill. I couldn't make it out.

'They're selling oxen,' she said. 'Clay oxen.'

Her voice calmed me. It made me feel foolish. There was a moment, then, in which I saw with complete detachment the little ox lying on its side on the palm stretched out to me. It was indeed made and baked from clay. It had horns. It had eyes scratched out with the end of a twig. The clay was reddish-brown and had in it the marks of thumbs that had tamped it into shape.

'How much?' I said.

'One cent, one cent,' screamed the voice in my left ear.

I looked from the ox to the hand that held it. I moved my eyes from the hand up the arm to the face at the window. We stared at each other.

'Children,' I observed stupidly. There didn't seem to be anything else to say. They were indeed children. But they were children dressed in the rags of an unutterable poverty. Shoeless and shivering, they stood like me at forsaken roadsides, crying for a single cent to weigh down their pockets or hands with something – anything – of substance.

'My God,' I said again. 'Buy one. Buy an ox.'

'No,' she said.

'A cent!' I shouted. 'Look at them, they're starving! What's a cent to you?'

'No,' she repeated, staring out at the tiny black faces peering with furious hope into the car.

With knotted fingers I pulled a five rand note from my pocket and pushed it out the window. It was all the money I had. In a violent scrambling the two children leaped at it and at each other. They fell to the ground at the edge of sight, tearing at and beating one another for possession of the grubby rectangle of paper. It was only as she pulled away that I realised I did not have even a clay ox to show for my impulsive charity. We bumped along the road now at reckless speed, jarring from side to side.

'Don't you care?' I said.

She said to me: 'Every cent you give them takes them further from desperation. They must be desperate,' she said, 'before the revolution will begin.'

We drove on for a little way in silence before she said, more softly than before, 'Five rand. You bastard.'

I'm not in search of a better world. How could I be when I run from things? I'm not crazy with dreams of progress and brotherhood and peace. People speak a great deal these days of The Struggle. What Struggle is this? I want no part in struggle. I understand only simple ideas. The most terrible thing about the Nazi era was that it made no exceptions. Not even for children. We *must* allow children to believe in things like happiness. If not in happiness, then in the *possibility* of happiness. I can put it no bettter than this (I don't want to grow old). Desperation should be reserved for old age. And what's five rand to me anyway?

She'd been there before, she knew the road. The campsite was a level field of lawn, hemmed in with tall fragrant trees. A short slope went down to a stream at the bottom edge of the grass. On all other sides one felt a brooding immensity indistinguishable from the darkness of the night. It was out of season and no other campers were there, but through the leaning trunks of trees one glimpsed still the trembling of the fires we had passed on the road. It was a clear night.

'You've left it late, haven't you?' I said, as we dragged the folded tent from the back of the car. But she didn't answer me.

We struggled to put up the tent. Fumbling in the yellow glow of a gas-lamp, we pushed and pulled till the skin of canvas was stretched across its steel skeleton. It was really too small for both of us. There was also only one stretcher. But after spending so many nights in the open, I was quite happy to sleep in a corner.

'Get out,' she said, 'while I change.'

I walked across a narrow plank bridge that spanned the stream and found myself on a dust road following the steepening incline of the land. A hundred metres further up a footpath led off to the left. I followed it and was almost immediately on the needled floor of a pine forest. Blue shadows rippled across the ground. I sat, hugging my knees, and let the forest breathe its green breath into my face.

After half an hour, I rose and retraced my steps. The tent was in the middle of the field, lit from inside as though it were burning.

Much later, when I was lying on my back in the corner, one hand behind my head, she sat up in her sleeping-bag and said:

'I know who you are.'

She knew who I was. Of course she did. But I couldn't even work up a faint alarm. Perhaps it was just that I was too tired, but I like to think that I trusted her with a fundamental trust that was completely strange to me. In any event, my mind remained numb. I had stripped down to my underwear and the lamp was cold across my skin. I studied the subtle shadows between my ribs. Then I cleared my throat.

'Yes?' I said.

'It's been in the papers,' she said. '*The Weekly Mail*. Your family's mad with worry.'

'No, they're not,' I said.

'They had your photo and everything. You were even on police file. Your father made a statement about that. He said something about how they were making you out to look like a criminal.'

'Really,' I said. 'I didn't know that.'

'Jesus,' she said, and there was glee in her voice. 'You showed them. You showed those bastards.' Then she kept quiet for a long while, so long that I found myself falling asleep. When she spoke again, it was with an insistence that made me roll onto my stomach to look at her. 'How did you do it?' she asked. 'Tell me how you did it.'

'I walked,' I told her.

'Bullshit,' she said. 'There's a desert to cross. And miles of bush. Please tell me.'

'I walked,' I said.

'The army had an inquiry.' I think she was talking to herself. 'They decided that you'd either been killed by

SWAPO or eaten by wild animals. Anything can happen up there. But you showed them. You showed those bastards. How did you do it? Please tell me how you did it.'

'I walked,' I said for a third time and now I was slipping away. Her voice was faint.

'Okay, so don't tell me. Keep it a secret. I guess that's your right. But tell me this: what do you plan now? Where do you want to go from here?'

'I don't know,' I mumbled and then my voice was extinguished. This time she let me sleep.

I opened my eyes on pale daylight coming in through the seams of the tent. Birds called and answered outside. She was still asleep, turned away under her blanket with one arm over her head. I crawled on cold-stiffened knees to the entrance and lifted aside the flap. I looked up at the mountains. I knelt in this way, insulated in a kind of white amazement, for a long time.

I had never seen such mountains before. In the first level rays of sun they were huge and static and grim. Mist was moving between the crags. I'm quite prepared to believe that man's lingering obsession with inhospitable regions like jungles, icelands and (dare I say it?) deserts, comes from spiritual equivalents to all these places in himself. But what barrier in me could ever equal this? I broke out in gooseflesh. I shivered.

But not for long. Within half an hour, when I'd dressed and made a fire, I was almost accustomed to the close cliffs teetering over us. I boiled water for coffee. As I crouched over the coals, holding the mug in my hands as hot as a gun, she came out of the tent. She was brushing her hair with little nervous strokes as she looked around her. 'Something, huh?' she said. 'I love the mountains. I come here as often as I can. I needed to come now ...'

She fell silent.

'Before what?'

But she didn't answer. She was by now also kneeling at the edge of the fire. There was a faint reflected glow, like a smear of red, under her eyes. She was staring at me, steadily and hard. She said, 'Did we wake you?'

'When?'

'Last night. Some people came round. We tried to be quiet. I hope we didn't …'

'No,' I said. 'I didn't wake.'

She continued to look carefully at me for a moment longer before dropping her eyes. I felt vaguely guilty for no reason at all. I thought back through my sleep, but could recall nothing, no wakeful moments in which there were voices or torches or bodies moving outside the tent. I looked around, hoping to see a footprint in the wet ground.

'You should get civilian clothes,' she said as she stirred milk over the fire. 'You're very obvious like that.'

'Where would I get civilian clothes?'

She squinted up at the sky. 'It's going to be a good day.'

'When are you leaving?' I said.

'Tomorrow morning.'

'Where are you going?'

'Back to Pretoria,' she snapped, then pointed with her spoon. 'Give me the cereal.'

'Why did you come here for one day?' I asked.

'Give me the cereal,' she said again, and I did.

We packed a picnic lunch in her rucksack and set out on a faint track through the same woods I'd rested in the night before. The sun was well up now and its yellow beams stood awkwardly between the trees like thick stalks of bamboo. Apart from the occasional dip, the path ran fairly steadily upwards, following the course of the stream that marked the lower edge of the campsite. We didn't talk much. The air was layered and heavy, vibrating with the noise of birds and the rattling of the waters in their stony bed. Every so often we stopped to rest, rubbing our thighs and gasping. All the while as we walked I kept my eyes on her back in front of me. I could see the pulse of muscles beneath her shirt. Higher and further the mountains hung on all sides. Eagles or vultures – I can't say which – stippled the sky.

After an hour or two the path left the forest and began to climb towards a gorge. The stream still flowed beside us. From there on the landscape changed markedly, losing any geographic constancy as it progressed. We ducked from grassland to forest to jungle to kloof. And other things began to happen. There were no more birds to be seen or heard. Only our feet, our breathing and the leaping water were audible in that whole hushed amphitheatre. Except for what must have been unfelt winds that piped high in the surrounding stone walls like distant jeering laughter. The precipitous crowns of the mountains were on every side. The air seemed darkened by them, although we were still in full sunlight.

And yet more things began to happen. In places the way was difficult to negotiate, going over rocks and bogs or simply climbing up too steeply. In these places I gave her my hand or shoulder for support and once even lifted her up a bank by her waist. Her grip was firm and feminine. Perhaps it was the altitude, but the higher we climbed the dizzier I became. I was conscious of an ever present fascination with the shapes of her, with the slight dry smell of her hair, with the delicate patches of sweat that glued her shirt to her shoulders and sides. I realized that I had possessed this fascination with her long before I'd ever seen her. She fitted pore for pore into an inconsolable space that had ached till then in my chest and groin. It was possible that I'd been running towards instead of away. It was possible that I'd reached the end of my road.

It must have been close to noon when we stopped. Shadows clustered beneath trees and bushes. It was certainly a fine place for a picnic. We sat on a sun-warmed sheet of rock beside a dark pool into which the stream spilled in a waterfall from some twenty feet up. We were both hot and had grown tired with this relentless walking. A slope cut off our view, but we were otherwise high enough to have looked out over the lowlands as they washed towards the sky. As it was, we could not see far on any side. We sat, our feet dangling in the icy water of the pool. I held her hand.

And, much later, we swam. I was not shy to leave all my clothes on the rock and climb naked into the pool. She joined me without hesitation. The water was freezing. It lined my skeleton with ice. I could see her breasts glimmering whitely beneath the surface and wanted to touch them. We kicked over to where the stream came down from above, hurling out pellets of water in a painful spray. The pool was deep, so deep that we couldn't feel the bottom. It felt eerie, that void beneath. She sensed it too.

'It's like something's waiting underneath to grab you,' she said.

So we swam back to the side and lay in the sun on our backs. Her pubic hair grew fluffy as it dried. I tried to eat a sandwich, but it was warm and unpleasant. The sky imprisoned us coldly from above. I thought of music and beer but they seemed absurd. I wanted. I needed. Wanted what? Needed what? Forget the sky. I felt far more imprisoned by the ridiculous construction of flesh, the arrangement of bones and hair and … the rest. Oh God. To touch. Just to touch.

'I'm also on a quest,' she said.

'For what?' I asked.

'Tomorrow,' she said dreamily, 'I am going to park a car full of explosives in Church Street in Pretoria.'

'Where in Church Street?' I whispered back.

She told me.

'But that's the army,' I cried.

'Yes.' She was whispering now too. (My cry was incongruous.) 'Yes. They'll all be lined up waiting for their afternoon buses. Bang.'

'No,' I said. 'Don't do it. Please don't do it.'

'Why not?'

'Please don't. Please come with me. Please stay with me. We'll go down to Durban and stow away on a ship. We'll sail to some other place where nobody needs a bang to change anything. Please …'

My voice trailed off. Of course I'd lied to her the previous evening. Of course I knew where I wanted to go. I was committed to trusting in some other land where children did not sell clay oxen at the side of the road. Some part of me forever approached this shore across acres of wind-chopped sea. But what ship could take me there? No ship from Durban harbour. At times I could well believe that this was an empty universe apart from tiny planet earth, that all the stars were waiting in uninhabited desolation for men to find and cover and blacken them till no refuge was left in skies or seas or space anywhere. Anywhere at all.

'No,' she said. 'Why don't you come with me?'

'They'll catch you,' I said. 'They'll catch you and hang you …'

'They won't,' she said.

'You're a coward,' I said. 'I know your type. I know you people. You plant bombs and run away. You're all cowards.'

She laughed at me. 'I'm going to be sitting in the car when it explodes,' she said. 'Come and sit with me.'

Oh yes. So that's it. But is this all that's awaited me through the short years of my life? Surely I was devised for better things. Or was I? What of all the other victims at the roadside with their briefcases and starched uniforms, furtively saluting one another, looking at the shoulders of approaching people rather than their eyes? With them I hear the explosion of the hidden bomb. I see the perimeters of my existence shrinking at incredible speed. I witness my own extermination converging on me from all sides. What right do I have to determine where the end of my road lies?

Later I left her drowsing on the rock, face down. Still unclothed, I made my way up through dense bushes to another pool at the top of the waterfall. There was a basin of rock and I leaned against its side. From there, by turning my head to the right, I could look down on her from above. Perhaps it was just the way the air quivered with heat, but there seemed to be an immense distance between us. Her buttocks were white and untanned. There was also a narrow strip of white across her shoulder-blades. Her hair lay partly across the side of her face. She hadn't seemed to register my leaving her side. For an instant I think I seriously contemplated a continuation of my flight, plunging up toward the source of the stream, reeling naked into the mountains on bruised feet. But the sight of her feather-fine body on the rock was enough to keep me there. I reached down and took myself in hand. It didn't need much. A few brief tremblings of the wrist and her form wavered before my eyes as though it lay beneath water. I spurted hotly against the crushing weight of the mountains.

And later still, washed clean, embarrassed, I strode in front of her on the long walk back to the tent. We were dressed once more, but my clothes felt strange on me. I was hardened by my days of movement, but my limbs hurt with fatigue as we came stumbling back to the campsite. She lit the gas-lamp. I put out deck-chairs on the grass. As the sun sank behind the mountains, deep shadows spilled from the gorge towards us. The air turned cool. We sat side by side, but I could not bring myself to hold her hand.

'Guy,' she said. 'Will you be coming with me tomorrow?'

'I don't think so,' I said.

After a long silence she said again: 'Guy?'

I didn't answer.

'Guy,' she said, so softly that I wasn't sure if she'd actually spoken. 'Guy, I think we should ...'

She didn't finish. But I knew what she meant. I had thought of nothing else since we'd swum naked in the icy water of the pool. But now no motion came. I knew that if I reached for her she would crumble in my fingers like bread. I twitched words from my mouth.

'What?' I said.

'Nothing,' she whispered. We sat on in the darkness, confined to our separate selves. Behind us those eternal mountains glowered, just as they had done when they confronted the bearded Voortrekkers in their wagons. But the graceless Boers had not been daunted. I saw them in my mind's eye as they shuddered and crashed over this trivial barrier that Africa had thrown up against the consuming tread of their oxen. Our heritage was no less ox-like in its solidity and stance. But then – so many oxen are made of clay. Above us the slow white torrent of stars wheeled imperceptibly across the sky. And down in the valley those red fires burned on, burned on.

RICK

His mother was a small woman, stocky as a snowman. She had bad teeth. Her nostrils were just too wide for her nose.

She would begin at the breakfast table: 'I was going to be a sculptor. I wasn't going to have a family. But when I met your father, he made me change my mind.'

'Joan,' Dad would say.

That was her name.

'Look at my hands,' she ignored him. 'These are the hands of a sculptor. I used to chip at stones with these hands.'

Her hands were like stones themselves, Shell thought, grey and rough, with mens' nails. The joints of her fingers were stony, too. He could hear them rasp when they moved. He could not see his mother chipping stones. It was hard to imagine her doing that.

'Your father rescued me from a life of stones,' she said. She laughed.

Behind their thick glass, he could feel that Dad's eyes were on him.

'The grass needs cutting,' he would say, as he poured orange juice in a neat stream. 'Perhaps, Shell ...'

'This afternoon,' he promised.

His mother licked the ends of her fingers and blinked at him.

'Thank you, Shell,' Dad said. He looked very good in a grey jacket. He had a plump briefcase that he carried too.

It gave Shell a strange joy to push the roaring mower over the passive green lawn. Small stones spat out sideways.

He would tie his shirt about his waist and move across the grass with the raw scent of torn blades breathing over him. The house was above, watchful. He could see the window of his bedroom.

He thought they were a normal family, which is to say that there was nothing remarkable about them: Shell, his sister Estelle and their two parents. They had lived for fourteen years in this stony cottage under thatch, with the high hills about. Shell could remember no other life. Nor could he conceive of a future that did not in some way include being young and here. He was happy to be so.

But his mother was not happy for him. She would try to change him:

'Shell,' she said. She pinched at the edges of her dress so that he could see her agitation. 'Shatsi ...'

He stood at the verge of the back stoep. Light was caught in the vine overhead; the slate was mossy with shadow. It was a clear day.

Avoiding her concerned gaze, he told her once again: 'I don't like to talk to people.'

'But Shatsi. Why not?'

'I just don't,' he said, picking at a leaf.

'That's not an answer. You have to learn. You have to work at being ...' Her sculptor's hands chopped at the air. 'Sociable,' she cried at last, and subsided into her dress. 'You have to be sociable.'

'I try.'

'Shatsi, you do not. You do not try. Would you say your behaviour yesterday was evidence of trying? Would you?'

Mrs Fynn was exasperated. A small burst of saliva came from her mouth and misted down to the slate. He watched it settle. The day before, Estelle had had some friends round for a braai; he had climbed out of his window rather than walk through the lounge and past them.

'They're older than me,' he said. His fingers were tearing the leaf now into tiny bits. He dropped them at his feet.

'Not all of them. Not all of them, Shatsi.'

'I don't care.' His obstinacy had brought him to tears; he bit at the inside of his lips.

'That is precisely the point. That is precisely what concerns me. It is impossible to talk to you, Shell ... I think I have a migraine coming on.'

She was prone to these. She would lock herself in her room for hours or days with the curtains drawn. Shell looked at her with interest, though still through tears. He could only picture her as she must lie in the dark room with a cloth upon her forehead, bulging with pain. 'I'm sorry,' he said.

'Oh, Shatsi,' she murmured. 'Will you try, Shatsi? For me? ... Just try, is all I'm asking ...' He didn't answer. 'It's because I love you,' she said viciously. 'Only because I love you.'

He let himself be kissed then, a bloodless blow between the eyes. Then she released him and was walking away over the cool slate. Her voice seemed to echo still, very faintly, to his ear; but it was only the hot shrieking of the cicadas in the valley below.

She sent his father to him a week later, where he lay on his bed upstairs, hands behind his head. Dad sat on the coverlet, half turned away. It was early evening, with the last of the light coming in through his window. It made the grey hair silver on the head of this man he hardly knew at all. The room about them had become a tiny terrain of stretched shadows and shapes wavering in the twilight. His desk, his bookcase, the old pine cupboard, all were melting towards the floor. Shell, with his tense hands cupped at the

curve of his head, looked at his father and saw him for a
jagged instant as if he'd never done so before: he saw a
middle-aged man, uncertain of himself, his face a hasty
assembly of bits. Large blue eyes under heavy brows; ears
entirely visible, not touched by hair; a mouth as prim as a
kitten's. And those hands clenched between his knees.
Delicacy did not come easily to Dad.

'We're only worried about you,' Dad said. 'It's for your
sake we're concerned.'

'I'm okay.'

'I'm sure you are.' He nudged his glasses up his nose,
although he didn't need to. 'What about school?'

'What about school? School's okay.'

'Do you have friends? Do you play with the other boys?
At … break … ?'

'Ja.' Shell decided to lie, if that would dispel these
demands. 'I play at break. I've got lots of friends at school.'

Dad sat, considering. His shoulder blades showed
through his shirt. 'Why don't they ever come here?'

'We live too far out. We're miles away from anything.'

'Estelle's friends come here. She has friends here every
Sunday.'

She did too, groups of gangly adolescents who sat about
on the back stoep, holding meat over a fire. Shell avoided
them. He even climbed out of windows to avoid them.

'I don't like people,' he said at last, and sighed for this
revelation to them both.

Dad turned his head to look at him, his large eyes larger
behind their lenses. His mouth was trembling. He almost
looked frightened as he stared down at his odd son lying on
the bed. He cleared his throat and said: 'That's no way to
talk. You know you don't mean that.'

'That's just the way I am,' said Shell, and rolled sideways

into the pillow. Bats tumbled silently outside the window.

They didn't speak about it again, at least not to him. He knew, though, that they watched him carefully from behind their curtains; from over their magazines; from beneath their eyelids.

Estelle never mentioned it at all. Estelle, in fact, hardly spoke to him about anything. She was a thin girl with hair a little less white than his. Her braces had come off a year before and now her teeth were perfectly straight. He'd noticed that she wore an occasional touch of makeup. Once or twice he'd come into the lounge and found her painting her nails. These dabs of colour she applied to her body fascinated him, though perhaps only because her manner had lost all hue. She did not – as before – consult or tease him. She shrugged off even his accidental caress. Sometimes still, to be truthful, she would pinch his arms as he passed, twisting his skin with cruel fingers. 'Pig,' she hissed through her even teeth. Then let him go.

It was difficult to believe that this was the same sister who, soiled and careless as he, would play every afternoon with him in the forests nearby. She hadn't cared about clothes or nails then.

Now she covered herself if he walked into the bathroom by mistake, one arm across her chest, the other slammed shut between her legs, squealing until he withdrew.

She was indifferent to his jealousy. He followed her at school from a distance. During break he would stand at the edge of the playground, kicking at stones, watching Estelle talking to her group of sycophants. Hands on hips, hair longer than it was allowed to be, she chewed gum and sniggered about teachers. Sometimes she even sniggered about him; he could tell by the way the circle of faces avoided looking in his direction, while they laughed and laughed. Their laughter made him blush, but it didn't drive him away.

Now, of course, that mocking group of friends was on the back stoep on Sunday afternoons. Estelle moved easily among them. From his bed he could hear her giggles drifting up to the window. She had become a hard shape with jutting things under her blouse. Tender red buttons appeared on her cheeks. He wasn't sure that he didn't hate her.

Early in the morning his mother would send him out to pick bananas or avocados for breakfast from the trees at the bottom of their property. He would stand with a thin mist rising from the still cold earth, while the first sun caught at the crests of the mountains. Above him the branches spilled skywards, their patterns as intricate and convulsive as his own. Sometimes he would go walking at twilight on the track down by the stream, when moths came blittering through the blue air. All around him the sweaty, steaming undergrowth was in quiet combat with itself; thorn on creeper on shoot on leaf. He thought he could hear groaning, if he tried.

It was a brutal land, all the more so because it was also fragile; he saw pylons going up between the trees. But there were still places that nobody else knew. Shell knew all the paths around (he'd made some of them himself) and where they joined. There were landmarks to keep him safe: the forester's hut at the top of the hill, always with smoke coming out the chimney; the stream at the bottom of the valley; the little dam at the beginning of the Nortjes' property. The mountains themselves gave direction – square onto the house were the cliffs; off to the right, angled towards town, the row of Disciples leered, their petrified grey faces forbidding. To the left was the Spear, its peak not as sharp as it looked from here. Curiosity had taken him there, and elsewhere, even occasionally out of the calm plantations, into forest that had not yet been cut. It was frightening, yes, but he liked to be alone.

In summer this was a humid place. A dank heat thickened the air. There was a rock slide far upstream where you could skid twenty metres on your bum into an icy pool, and lie afterwards on warm stone while the sun dried you. But winter was too cold for that. Autumn and spring were not very evident to the eye, here where green was a constant colour. But there were other indications of change that one could feel. And smell. Shell carried in him the memory of scents that could pare time away without warning: woodsmoke; the fragrance of crushed leaves; the vile odour of rotting meat (a dead dog in the woods). Even water had a clean tang to his nose.

Dad had been a sportsman when he was young. He'd tried to teach Shell. On the back lawn in the evenings, after he'd come home from work, they would stand and throw a ball to each other. Shell clutched in the air for the round shape that flew towards him. But his hands were webbed; they clashed; the ball flew aside and hit the lawn.

'You must watch the ball, Shell. All the way into your hands.'

'I do.'

'You don't. You close your eyes at the last minute. You can't miss if you watch.'

He ran through the glossy air to catch the ball. He ran with happy panic, reaching not for the circle of leather but for the approval of the man who stood at the other end of the lawn, hands on hips, watching.

'Better. Better.'

'I kept my eyes open.'

'You should practise. You should join a team at school and play.'

'I might,' he said, lying, as he threw the ball back. And his mother stood on the stoep behind her square skirt and shrieked when he missed. 'Watch!' she called. 'Listen to your father!'

'I am!'

'You're not! I can see from here you're not!'

'Leave him, Joan,' Dad said. 'Leave him alone.'

Shell was grateful to him for his weary support. He wished that he could be in teams for him, to make him proud. It was a consolation that Dad was not a sportsman anymore and looked as though he'd never been one; he moved too slowly now, and heavily. Dad was a pharmacist. He worked with drugs. All day long he poured careful measures of fluid from tube to tube; perhaps for this reason, his delicate hands could not be hard. His mother would hit Shell sometimes, a cuff with her knuckles at the back of the head. But Dad could never hit, not ever.

Not even the time with the chocolate.

'I didn't.'

'Then where? Where did you get it? Shell?'

He couldn't answer. They were in the car – the white Triumph his mother used – at the side of the main street in town. Shell held the melting chocolate bar, just opened, in his fist. He stared at it as if it might explain itself to him.

'Did you take it, Shell?' Dad's voice was bubbly. Shell wondered if he was going to cry. 'Did you take it from the café? Did you?'

He didn't answer. He let his silence become an admission, because they both knew anyway. It had been a meaningless deed for him in the dusty shop, while his father's back was turned at the counter. It hadn't been criminal, merely a yielding to shiny paper under his hand. Only as his fingers returned to his pocket had the reaching out become an act, and even then not irreversible. There were only short steps needed to undo his motion. If he had to.

'Why, Shell?' Dad had his arm around his shoulders now. It was this gentleness that frightened him, when he had expected blows. 'Tell me why.'

'I wanted it.' A simple truth he couldn't fault.

'Don't you understand that you ... you can't *take* whatever you want?'

Shell frowned at the chocolate, which was melting onto his hand now.

'Don't you understand that it isn't yours? It doesn't belong to you.'

'He didn't see me.' For the first time Shell turned his head to look into his father's eyes. He was wrong; there were no tears there.

'It doesn't matter if he didn't see you. It doesn't matter if nobody saw you. Not even me. What matters is that you *did* it. Shell? You did it.'

Shell was unconvinced, but he didn't argue. He was more fascinated by this troubled face at his shoulder. Dad had blackheads on the tip of his nose.

'You must go and give it back, Shell.'

'Me?'

More terrible than the anticipated blow: an abyss had opened in the car. Shell clutched at the seat. The chocolate fell into his lap and he grabbed blindly at it. When he raised his head again his eyes shone with tears. *Me.* He saw himself staggering back inside, the fat figure of Mr Kakoulla behind his counter. The Greek would bend to hear his faint voice, smiling at this timid child who had some message to relate. Until he heard him; until he was betrayed by Shell's confession. He began to sob into his sleeve. His helpless father watched.

'Shell –'

'I *can't!* Dad ... I'm sorry ... Please ...'

'Don't cry. Look ...'

'I can't. I can't ... Don't make me. Please. I'll never do it again ... *Please.*'

'*Shell* –'

At which point Shell swung out a directionless fist, the blow perhaps his father had failed to deliver. He hit Dad in the face. His glasses spun off, landing at his feet; his hands came up to his nose. For a moment they sat side by side, neither moving, both horrified at an event Shell didn't understand. Then he lunged at him. Shell hugged his father's chest, his ribs against his cheek, tears running into his shirt. Dad patted his head.

'Dad ... I'm sorry ... I ...'

'All right.'

He pushed Shell firmly away. Contact embarrassed him. He fumbled for his glasses and examined them carefully before putting them back on.

'Dad ... I'm sorry.'

'All right. All right.'

Shell continued to cry, though, as his father started the car and moved out into the street. He saw this unpleasant little town – cramped and tiny, close to the ground – through spilling water. But as they headed back towards the road that would take them to the hills and home, they began to leave behind the towering Greek at his till. Shell grew quiet. They drove in silence. He unwrapped what remained of the chocolate bar. He looked at his father, but no sign, no glance, passed between them. He licked his fingers when he'd finished eating.

He wasn't sure whether his mother ever knew about the incident. It was difficult to tell what his mother knew about him. At unexpected times she would seize him, wrestle him in her jointless arms smelling of powder. 'Shatsi,' she would croon between kisses that left wet patches on his forehead. 'Shell, darling.' Then she'd let him go, her bosom kicking like something alive under her dress.

There was a time when he'd not been able to help himself. 'Leave,' he shouted, his voice so raw that it shocked him too. 'Leave me alone!'

She stood back, his mother, aghast, her hands shaking. 'It's only love,' she said.

'I hate it when you touch me. I hate it.'

'Oh, Shatsi,' she hissed, 'it's just that I don't want you to be like your father. I wouldn't want that.'

He couldn't think what she meant. There was nothing the matter with Dad. He did not treat her badly; he would sit with nodding patience across the table from her, placate her with his voice. It was she who shrieked. It was she who threw the plate that time across the kitchen, so that it smashed against the door and showered little bits into Dad's hair.

'Joan,' he'd said. 'I don't want this ... in front of the children.'

His voice was dull. It was the colour of old bricks, baked in the sun for years and years.

'The children,' she said.

'Joan.'

'Give me a life,' she said. 'You owe me a life.' There was steam coming up from the sink behind her; grey steam rising like mist from the marshy sink.

No, Dad was good to her. There was only once that it

might have been otherwise. Shell was woken in the night. There were cries and sounds of struggling from inside the house. He got up, unafraid because only half-awake, and went down the passage on giddy feet. His father and mother had separate rooms; it was late; the noises were coming from his mother's room. He knew this before he got there, before he saw. Peering through the crack of the open door, he witnessed a tussle unlike any other he had seen. His mother and father clobbered at each other like sacks of meat; savage; intent; a collision he could never ask them about. He looked for blood, but could see none. So he went back to his room. He lay in his bed and felt the blood dripping from these walls instead. It was a long time before he went back to sleep.

They were normal again in the morning. He was reassured by the breakfast table, and by daylight. They all sat about and ate toast.

He was hungry; he'd been afraid he never would be again.

Breakfast table conversations were the ones he remembered best. Words lay on the table amongst the plates.

'You're messing on your shirt,' his mother said. 'Eat nicely, Shatsi.'

'Don't *attack* your food,' Estelle said. She didn't look at him.

'Leave him, Estelle.' Dad sometimes used with Estelle that same weary voice that he used with his mother.

It was his mother speaking now. 'Listen to your father, Estelle. You should respect your father. Your father, make no mistake, is a man worthy of respect.'

'Joan.'

They faced each other over the top of the table, which

was littered like a battleground.

'Have you packed your books, Shatsi?'

'Yes,' Shell said. 'I did it last night.'

'Don't talk with your mouth full.'

'Leave him, Estelle.'

'No,' his mother said. 'Never be afraid to speak. Always speak out, Estelle. Speak out before it's too late.'

'It is never,' said Dad, 'too late.'

'Listen to your father. Your father is a wise man. Your father,' she announced, 'has ruined my life.'

'You have your life,' he said.

Shell drank his orange juice, tilting the fierce liquid down his throat, with the sound of glasses, knives, forks, chipping carefully away on all sides. It was a quarry, his home.

His mother was laughing in her chair. She sat, a dab of marmalade on her sleeve, with yellow gobbets of laughter falling from her mouth. 'I have my life,' she said. 'Children, do you hear? I have my life.'

In the evenings the family would watch television. Shell liked to watch television; it meant that there was no need to speak. His family, finally and safely silent, sat about him in a half circle, their faces stupefied with concentration. They watched commercials, interviews, sit-coms, dramas.

One night he sat eating popcorn and staring at a wildlife documentary. Creatures in the wild, the television informed, existed on their senses alone. Sight, hearing, smell, touch, taste – these were what allowed animals to explore their environment, to defend themselves against their enemies, to hunt their own prey. They used camouflage to outwit the senses of their foes and their food. Shell watched with increasing horror the movements of beasts and insects. He watched chameleons creeping down branches, shooting their tongues at flies. He watched eagles plummeting out of the sun. He was appalled. Abruptly, without warning, this square, contained vision spilled from its box; it spread in concentric rings that burst from the house and scythed away into the dark. The world was a forest of moving flesh that fed on other flesh; crawling and inching and loping closer or away. In terror he rose to his feet, knocking the bowl of popcorn from his lap. The white pellets sprayed.

'Shell! Be careful, Shatsi.'

'Jesus. Look at him.'

Dad was staring. 'What? Shell? What's the matter?' But he was already gone, running through the kitchen, through the outside door, into the clustering night. His skin prickled. He'd grazed his shin on the table as he passed. Motion left him slowly as the house and its lighted windows receded behind. But he only stopped running when he was halfway up the road. Now – it seemed for the first time ever – he was completely still, enclosed in the sighing blackness. Trees hung breathless over him. Through their branches he could see stars, remote and high. He stood with his arms folded across his chest, clutching at himself, a trembling form at the side of a deserted road. Fear continued to spread in rings from a core within him too deep for his hands. His body ached, as if already rent by teeth.

They decided to send him away.

'But why?'

He stood with his hands behind his back. They faced him on the couch, side by side. They looked earnest, as though they were courting him, or each other.

'It is for the best,' his mother said.

'We have given it a lot of thought. You must believe that.' Light from the lamp made Dad's glasses opaque. Shell could see nothing behind them.

'But I don't *want* to!' He was already close to tears.

'Why? Tell me why.'

'It can't be good,' said Dad. 'So far from the city …The new school will be good for you.'

'You're going into high-school now, Shatsi. It is the time to make a new start.'

'But I don't want to make a new start. You didn't send Estelle away.'

Dad stirred, a slow, scaly movement. A reptile on a rock. He licked his lips with a split tongue. 'We're not sending you away, Shell. Don't twist our words. We feel … your mother and I … we feel it would be better for you to be in a boarding-house. We – '

'Why? Why will it be better?' Shell was crying now, without attempting to conceal it. Tears so hot they put out his eyes. His nose was running too.

'We've given it a lot of thought,' his father said again. He was upset by this display of emotion. Any emotion upset him.

With difficulty, his father conceded: 'We feel … your mother and I … that you're too introspective. You need to mix more with people, people of your own age, Shell.'

There was a pause. His mother was crying now too. She was pummelling her nose with a pink tissue. 'We went to speak to your teachers, Shell,' Dad went on. 'They say you don't mix at all, that you don't seem to have any friends.'

'And Estelle, Shatsi. She says you stand around by yourself at break. She says –'

Shell was amazed at the extent of their treachery. He no longer cried. Staring at them through tunnels of red, he wiped his mouth with the back of his hand. They looked at him in consternation.

Dad tried again: ' … for your own good … your mother and I … only want the best. For you. You know that.'

Turning to the window, Shell looked out into a congealing dark that reflected his own. They stared at him while he looked away.

At last he accused: 'It's the ball. Isn't it? It's because I couldn't catch the ball.'

His father blinked, as though he truly could not understand. But Shell was not deceived.

'I think I have a migraine coming on ...' His mother propped up her forehead with her fingers. Otherwise her head would have fallen from her neck, a heavy glass globe, and smashed on the floor. He willed it so.

'You will understand,' his father said, 'if you give it a little thought.'

He understood already. Words welled up to the surface of his tongue. But he doubted very much that he would ever speak to them again. His beloved parents.

After his father had left the room, his mother grabbed at him. Her face was guttering in a sudden wind. He didn't resist this time as she clawed him, snapping his bones in her voracious embrace. She kissed his forehead. 'Shell ... Shell, darling ...' She let him go, or fell away.

His last weeks at home were parched and endless. He continued to roam through the forests nearby. But now everything upon which his gaze fell became illuminated by a clear white light that had its origin in him. Trees, leaves, folds in the ground; all blazed in the pure pain of his sight. He walked upright, stiffly, careful not to spill what he was carrying.

There was no earthquake. Home and mountains didn't tremble, let alone shift in devastation. Yet silently, at the roots of his hair, this entire landscape was pouring and roaring with inexorable force.

He packed his belongings. He could not conceive of how

quietly the lock on the suitcase would close. It had barely taken an hour to fit his clothes into this allotted space. He had everything that he required. Underwear, socks, jeans; T-shirts. Two pairs of shoes. He had a little red sack that contained all his toiletries. His mother had put a tin of deodorant under his shirts. Neither of them mentioned it, because he hadn't used it before. He had his own comb, with strands of his hair woven into the teeth. And his blue toothbrush, which he hardly ever used. He didn't pack any books, for fear that he might be mocked.

He didn't say goodbye to Estelle. She was in her room, the door closed. He walked past without hesitation, his suitcase weighing down his right arm.

His mother and father drove him down to the station. His mother was to accompany him on the first trip; she had a little overnight bag of her own. He didn't recall that anybody spoke on the short drive downhill. The headlights of the car moved ahead, white and crazy. He sat on the back seat with his feet together.

Shell stood at the window as the train jolted underneath. Metal squeaked as it tightened and dragged, beginning to move forward and away. His fingers reached up to touch the glass, but were in fact trying to reach further; to reach the sombre, mourning face of his father outside as he started to trot to keep pace with him, down the grimy concrete of the station. Although his mother sat behind him in the close compartment, it was an emptiness he sensed at his back, also gathering momentum on clicking wheels. Between these voids, he moved away into dark.

Shell moved from class to class. He wrote in books. He was bored. During breaks he dashed back to the hostel to pack his books for the next three periods. His uniform was stiff and new. It was also uncomfortable; wet patches formed under his arms. He polished his shoes nightly, because that was the rule. He liked his reflection in the full-length mirror at the end of the dorm, and he learned to do his tie himself. He kept his blazer buttoned. Uniforms had always appealed to him, although he would not have been ready to admit it. In the library he found a book in which there was a photograph of Germans marching in the Second World War. They had tall black boots that shone. They had gloves. Their hair was as white as his, their eyes as blue. He longed to be marching with them to a glorious music.

Instead he was shambling around these dusty grounds. Over weekends there was too much time. He threw stones at the trunks of trees. He stood at the gate and looked out at forbidden soil beyond. If you climbed onto the big rock there and stretched, you could see the buildings in the city. They were stacked together like the funnels of some insidious engine beneath. Light shone off their windows.

Shell came to know the names of the other boys with whom he shared the dormitory, but learning their names only made them less strange; it did not make friends of them. In the shower at night he stood in a waxy thicket of flesh, trying not to tremble. The air was drumming with mist in which he could hear voices calling, but which, for all his roaming, kept him lost.

The dormitory was a long room with windows set into the walls at regular intervals. There was a bed beneath each window, and a tall green locker beside each bed. The floor was tiled with neat red tiles; the walls were clean with paint. When Shell had first arrived he stood in the doorway, his suitcase against his knees, and looked. It took a moment before he saw the others – figures sitting on the beds, leaning against lockers. But they had no substance against the white paint; they wavered as he looked at them. And, as far as they were concerned, he was ghostly too. They barely glanced at him where he stood. They barely glanced up with their soft white faces.

Shell took a bed at the end of the row, because he liked the wall on one side. He didn't unpack his suitcase. He lay down on the bed and looked directly upward with his eyes. There were faint grey marks in the ceiling that might have been made by water once. In their foggy patterns there seemed to be the contours of a face that never quite became solid; whose face he didn't know. Why it should be here, swirling just below the surface of the ceiling, he also didn't know. But he lay and searched for its elusive features. As he lay and looked, he could hear a thin and distant sound. There was a courtyard outside the window behind him; in this courtyard were four steel racks used for drying clothes. Although they were bare now, these structures were turning and turning in the wind, with high perpetual screaming in his ears.

'Like dyin'.'

He heard the voice, but wouldn't look. He didn't want to talk.

But the voice persisted. 'Don'tcha think ...?'

There was a boy on the next bed. Their eyes met. Although Shell looked away, it was too late.

'Hello.'

He looked back again to find this other one reaching out a hand. It could be for no one other than himself. He sat up. Wanting to claw at it, Shell shook the hand.

'Hello,' Shell said.

'I'm Rick.'

He waited.

'I'm Shell,' he had to say. Blood was fierce in his eyes.

'I'm also new here,' said Rick. His voice was too keen; it carried in the quiet.

The rest were staring at them. Even if he didn't look, Shell knew they were staring. As now –

'You mustn't be scared,' Rick was telling him. His eyes were rolling. 'It's not a bad place. I'll help you if you ... if you need help. I will,' he finished desperately.

Rick's lips, perhaps, carried a trace of foam. Anyway, Shell was able to lie back on his bed with a quite definite sneer. The absurd, anguished boy on the next bed was forced to do the same. His breath still sounded, though, quick and shrill.

It comforted Shell to have the friend he required. And so soon. Certainly he was no longer afraid. Grief is stronger than fear, maybe; and he had good cause for grief. He was, of course, an orphan. By the time a stern figure appeared in the doorway with a list of names in his hand, Shell Fynn had ceased to be daunted by this strange room and these strange boys. His skin had mottled to the gentle shade of the blanket upon which he lay. He was no longer visible to the naked eye.

In time, he wrote:

Dear Mom and Dad

I am in a dorm with twelve other boys. I don't know all their names yet, but one of them is – Rick. He sleeps in the next bed to me. The beds are hard. Also the seniors push us round. I am a skiv, that means I have to work for one of the form fives. I have to make his bed and polish his shoes. But I don't mind really.

He is quite nice to me.

I am lonely here, I wish I wasn't here. I cried last night. Please write soon. The teachers are okay, mine are anyway. I will write again next week.

In fact he hadn't cried the night before. In fact it was Rick in the next bed whom Shell had woken to find sobbing into his pillow. He got up and padded across the cold floor.

'Rick,' he said. 'Rick. What's the matter?'

But he was snorting and snuffling. Shell could see his shoulders heaving. He sat on the bed and touched at him. He put a hand on his back.

'Rick,' he said. 'What? Rick?'

Rick rolled suddenly over and stared. Shell withdrew his hand.

After a moment, Rick said, 'I hate it here. I don't wanna be here.'

But he'd stopped crying. His face in the near-dark was wizened and wrinkled. He was about to crumble.

There was a silence. Then Shell, amazed at how easily this came to him, gathered Rick up in his arms. For a very short moment there was an awkwardness between them, then Rick went slack, as though instantly and completely asleep. He brought up his hand and with a curved thumb plugged up the circular hole of his mouth. Shell held this head against his chest, the rough hair like grass against his palms. He rocked. 'Quiet,' he said, speaking on a low electric hum that soothed them both. 'Shhh ... quiet now ... quiet ...' They rocked together in the fine blue moonlight that came drifting in like spray. Nobody else was awake, but it was a sight that would have alarmed them if they were: the swaying pair on the bed, bound together in this bizarre embrace.

As he rocked, Shell too felt a kind of sleepy calm closing over his sight. He was holding in his hands all that was weakest and most despicable in himself. He could conceivably expiate himself, it seemed.

The boarders were required to participate in at least one

sport a term. Shell signed up for cross-country running in the afternoons. Every afternoon at four a little group would assemble on the athletics track. Golden light came from the sky at this time. The fields and trees were washed in it, becoming foreign, English. Shell felt serene.

They ran six kilometres each day. Sometimes, accompanied by a master, they would leave the school grounds and jog through the surrounding suburbs. By the time they returned to school, the day was beginning to taper. The forms of objects – fences, poles, walls – were dark on the air. Shell put on his tracksuit and walked towards the tap, the smell of grass in his nose. Rick fell in beside him. 'Good run,' he said.

'Ja. Okay. You're quite fit.'

'Naah. I got cramps. I got a cramp here.' He pinched at his thigh. 'I hate running,' he said.

'So why d'you do it?' Shell looked sideways at this skinny boy with short dark hair. Rick had a slight lisp. His head was shaped like a lantern, and looked like it might break as easily.

'I have to,' Rick said.

They bent in turn to drink, cupping the water and slurping. Shell stood afterwards with a trickle going down his chin. He laughed suddenly, for no reason clear to himself. Perhaps it was just the day, fading so gently. The sound of a train carried from over the road. He felt moved to mutter: 'I thought I was gonna hate it here. I thought it was gonna be horrible.'

Rick glared. 'It is. It is horrible here. Y'don't like it – the boarding-house?'

'It's okay,' Shell said.

'Don't you miss home?'

'I don't think about home.' He rubbed at the water on

his chin.

'Your mother and father ...'

'My mother and father were killed.' Shell wasn't looking at Rick; he was staring out over the cricket field to the grandstands. So was surprised to turn back to this horrified face, mouthing on mumbles. Rick could hardly speak. Shell smiled in alarm and reassured: 'I'm only joking. Not really. They're alive.' He started to walk up the tar in the direction of the hostel.

They ran together every day. Shell didn't have breath to talk, but it was pleasant to have Rick gasping alongside.

There were often times, even when he wasn't running, that there was nothing to say. They walked in the school together. Or sat on the steps out front drinking coffee.

'What do you want to do when you leave school?'

'I don't know.' The question didn't penetrate Shell. He sucked on a piece of grass. 'It's far away.'

'Not so far. Only four years.'

'Then army.'

'My brother's in the army,' Rick said. 'He's at Upington.' He sounded proud. Shell said: 'So?'

'I was just saying.'

Rick could be irritating.

They went walking up on the hill, throwing pine-cones between the trees. Their hands became sticky.

'I haven't ever had a friend before, Shell,' said Rick. 'You're the first friend I've ever had.'

Shell was touched and scornful. He swung at a cone with a broken branch. Their collision sent the cone in a long spinning arc. It crashed into bushes.

Rick persisted. 'We must of known each other in another lifetime. My mother believes in things like that. We must of been friends before.' He groaned with happiness at the thought. 'You mustn't tell anybody, Shell, but I've got an undescended tes-tikkel. That's a secret.'

'A what?'

'Look.' And Rick, after glancing around carefully, pulled open the front of his pants to show him. Shell was amazed.

'Does it hurt?'

'Yes.' After a moment, he conceded: 'No. Not really.' He closed his pants. 'I told you a secret. Now you tell me one.'

But Shell was throwing pine-cones again, as if he couldn't have cared. 'I don't have secrets,' he said. Even his voice was careless.

'I don't know anybody like you, Shell.' Rick was moaning. 'You stare at people. You frighten people.'

Shell had an urge to hit at the head of this miserable boy who was his friend. He would have liked that too; to see Rick's head flying between the trees.

'Shell? I get so lonely sometimes. I don't like to be with people, they don't feel like they're really there ... I don't like people. They can do things to you, people can.' He was grabbing at Shell, although his hands were at his sides. His voice was keen and thin. 'We're two of a kind, Shell,' he said. 'You and me. Two of a kind.'

Shell was likely to agree, but never aloud. He looked at the other, standing under the trees with his eyes blinking. It was a pitiable creature, this skinny, lisping Rick. 'You're silly,' Shell said. 'You say silly things.'

Rick was hurt. 'I only *meant* ...' he said. He was about to bawl.

'Let's go back,' Shell said, before he could. 'Let's go back to the house. It's getting late.'

It was a slow and easy time, after all. Shell didn't mind the roads and trees as much as he thought. When eight weeks had passed, they were allowed to take their first weekend off. But it was a long way home and Shell wasn't sure that he wanted to go. His mother and father were expecting him; they'd written to say how much they looked forward: ... *We miss you most at night, Shatsi, when we're all together here* ... Perhaps for this reason, Shell was compelled to write:

Dear Mom and Dad

You were right after all, this place is good for me. I hate it here but I am enjoying it. There's always something happening here. The things we do. You wouldn't believe. But I'm sorry, I won't be coming home on the fifteenth after all. I have a friend, Rick, he is in the dorm with me. I am going home with him on the fifteenth. He lives in Pretoria, only an hour away. I am looking forward to it.

Rick and me are two of a kind. He is nice, but he can make you angry. He says he doesn't believe in angels, but he believes in devils. You wanted me to have a friend.

Rick's mother was old. She was as shrunken as a grandmother, it seemed to Shell. She was thin, with the kind of thinness that revealed her skeleton under skin and clothes. She had grey hair in which you could see the last traces of a splendid black. When she fetched them at the bus-stop in Brooklyn, she wore a white garment that could have been a robe. Her fingers carried rings as bright as scabs.

It was a strange weekend. Rick lived in an outlying suburb, in a house that belonged to no suburb at all. The garden was dense and overgrown and appeared not to have been touched by a gardener's hands. Inside, the rooms were crowded with bizarre items of spiritual significance. There were drapes that were full of moons and wands and shapes. A crystal ball – it truly was – stood on a table in the lounge. A thick, cloying scent hung everywhere like fog.

'My mother,' Rick explained, 'is a spiritualist.'

His father lived elsewhere, alone. Perhaps he drifted somewhere in the house, but he seemed an unnecessary presence in the process that had produced Rick and his home. Only Rick's mother, with her heavy robes and flat shoes, was everywhere. She found Shell on Saturday night on the back lawn.

Abruptly, she said, 'Rick – you must treat him well. He's weaker than you are.'

'Yes,' Shell said.

'Good,' she said. She walked away towards the house, with her white robes following. He could hear her footsteps after all.

He and Rick did very little that weekend that was of significance to a mutual dependence. They sat about and read comics. They drank sour cooldrink from glasses. But it was enough to be there; to lie in separate beds across the room from each other. The wind could be heard outside. Rick had trusted Shell with knowledge; of his barmy mother, of their house full of occult crap. So that in a way those two days were a resolution. Not of their friendship, which was only a reason at best; but of the cruelty for which Rick hoped. They did in fact need each other.

On Sunday night they returned to the hostel. While they waited in the dorm before chapel, Rick just out the shower, a towel around his waist, Shell turned where he lay on the bed, turned, to the others where they sat or stood, in those same attitudes of perpetual waiting he recalled from his first arrival. He pointed at Rick an accusing finger.

'Hey,' he said. He had their attention. 'He's only got one *ball*,' he said.

Rick was white. He stared at Shell. 'You said you wouldn't say…'

They were laughing, the others. 'Really?' they wanted to know. 'Show us. Is it true?' They crowded him.

Rick held onto his towel.

They laughed then and Shell laughed too, with bitterness. He laughed as he betrayed the mad old woman, and himself.

It was the others that took pity when they saw tears in Rick's eyes. They left him alone and went back to their vigil. In their boredom they hardly glanced as Rick had to take off the towel to dress.

Shell watched, though. He refused to look away from blushing Rick with his undescended *tes-tikkel*.

'I'm sorry,' Shell said. He was. 'I didn't know you were so soft.'

There were no limits to Shell's hatred of the friend he also – surely – loved. From time to time, at unexpected moments (as they sat down at the swimming pool, or down at the cricket pavilion, watching a game), he would strike out at Rick with delight, hitting him in the stomach, making him double over. Or he'd grab his hair and pull till he snivelled. Mostly, though, it was the mortal blows he dealt when nobody else was near: 'I wish I'd never met you.'

'You don't!'

'I do. You're boring, Rick. You make me bored.'

Rick was abject, humble. 'I know I'm not good enough for you, Shell –'

'Yes, you are.' Shell crushed him 'You're good enough for me, Rick. Nothing special about me.'

They were inseparable. They walked to and from class together. They sat beside each other in prep, in morning assembly, at the supper table. Once a week on Wednesday afternoons the boarders were allowed to go into town. Rick and Shell went to movies. They saw *Endless Love*. They saw *First Blood*. They went to bookshops together. They bought ice-creams at shopping centres and wandered around, gazing into windows.

Shell never returned to Rick's home for another weekend. He feared the revenge of those grasping fingers, coated in rings. He might be smothered in those white robes.

Rick did ask once. 'Is it my mother?' he wanted to know. 'Does she frighten you?'

'I like your mother,' Shell said. 'If you must know, Rick, if you really have to know – it's you. I can't bear you. For too long at a time,' he added kindly.

Rick lowered his eyes.

'And nobody could blame me for that,' Shell said.

He understood so much. Rick thought he had never met anybody who understood so much. He would stare at Shell when he was looking elsewhere. It seemed to Rick that any amount of activity was pointless when there was Shell Fynn doing something elsewhere. He would wake up in the night and look at him. He would follow him anywhere.

Even into that dark hollow under the trees at the edge of the rugby fields. Light came down like a grey pollen. Rick squatted there, obliging, turned to look out through the hanging leaves toward the far field, where boys were running. Only to feel it hit his back. Only to feel Shell Fynn pissing on his back. He knew before he saw what was happening to him; he had himself conspired for this moment. For the hot, salty, contemptuous stream on his shoulders.

'Hey,' Rick cried. 'Hey, hey!' He was trying to get away. But not too hard.

Rick whimpered. Shell was also whimpering. Or perhaps

he was laughing, it was hard to tell.

When he was finished, he just stood. By this time Rick was sobbing. He was tearing at the ground. 'No,' he cried. 'No, no!' He threw sand. Urine stank in his hair. It stuck his shirt to his back.

Shell felt obliged to hold him. He knelt beside him and cradled him, rocking. They swayed together under the grey trees. They clung to each other. Rick saw that Shell was, actually, crying.

'I hate you. I hate you.' Rick could hardly talk.

But Shell, whose vindication was finally complete, felt only compassion.

At the end of the first term, Shell returned home for three weeks of holiday. It was with a dull reluctance that he boarded the evening train, wearing his school uniform and carrying the same suitcase with which he'd left. Only as the swaying carriage took him beyond the northern limits of the city did he begin to feel at ease. (Rick had left for Pretoria earlier that same day; he'd held onto Shell's sleeve. 'I wish I could go with you,' he said. 'You can't,' Shell said. 'I wish you'd come with me then,' he said. 'No, thank you,' Shell said. He had never felt such indifference. Rick had become an absence). Shell settled back into his seat and rolled his white sleeves up to his elbows. There were neat moles on the backs of his arms. A round wart had begun to form on his right hand, at the bottom of his thumb. He picked at it and thought. He thought of his mother who would be there to fetch him the next morning.

She was waiting on the platform. He saw her as the train moved in.

He saw her before her searching eyes saw him. She was a small woman, her skirt pulled sideways by the wind. For a moment he could not bring himself to recognise her. She was unknown, slight and odourless, not worthy of his resentment. He would have found it possible to walk past her without a second glance.

But she seized him as he stepped from the train, his suitcase in hand. She sucked his cheek with her dry lips.

'Shell,' she gurgled. 'Shell, darling.'

They drove to the house in the same white Triumph she'd owned since his memory began. The landscape passing at the windows — near and far, the signposts and trees, the views down the valley — was the same that he recalled from countless such drives into town and back. And coming down the rutted dirt road, the tyres buffeted below, he saw at the same bend the same glimpse of the roof below, between the trees.

He stepped out into the garage. He took his suitcase from the back seat. His mother walked ahead of him into the cool kitchen. He followed unwillingly.

'Your room, Shatsi. The very same.'

He climbed the stairs. His room was, indeed, unchanged; he glanced at the walls to see the tiny smudges he recalled. On his desk stood the tubular blue vase, holding its fistful of dry stems. He unpacked his clothes. He changed into shorts and T-shirt. He went back downstairs. His mother brought a tray of tea to him on the back stoep where he sat for the rest of the afternoon, watching the light burn away like a slow fuse. He barely moved on the chair. Above the mountains there was a smeary disc rolling, that people called the moon.

As always, it was the table that united them. Called by the round note of the bell, they congregated there while the night began outside. The knives and forks lay shining with sharp points and edges. He took his place.

His father sat opposite in his usual seat. Perhaps his hair was cut a little differently, or had begun to thin. Otherwise it was the very man that Shell could have conjured in his head; large, ponderous, the light gleaming off his glasses. He sawed at the chicken so that white chunks of meat fell away. His hands were just as white.

Estelle greeted Shell with hesitation. He answered gladly. She'd cut her hair and it curled over her ears and collar. She'd had an ear pierced. He sensed her on his left as a faint heat; his arm brushed hers once as he brought the fork up to his mouth.

'We're very pleased to have you home,' Dad said. There was a trickle of gravy from his mouth. It ran out like blood.

'So pleased, Shatsi,' his mother echoed, and raised her glass.

Estelle said nothing, but looked coyly down at her plate. With her fluttering eyelids she was wooing him, her conquering brother who had returned.

Afterwards he went back out to the stoep. An autumnal chill made the air stiff against his face. He leaned against a pole, wound with creeper. Without turning, he heard his father walk out behind and stand. Silent, they both looked down the dark valley, above which that moon had now become harsh and cold.

'We are, you know,' his father said. 'Very glad. To have you back.'

'Yes,' he said.

'You are always in our thoughts.'

He said nothing. He shifted against the pole and heard the fragile creeper tearing under his shoulder.

They stood, not speaking. The bald moon was pasted to the sky, as round and white as a cigarette burn. Shell had read that there were footprints marked indelibly on its surface. But down here in the lonely garden, he could not imagine those distant tracks. Here the trees were roaring in an unfelt wind. The same high stars were burning.

Shell left again two days before school started. The trip down to the station was a repetition of the last: the quiet car, headlights, dark. But he was absolutely without sadness as he took his leave. Fumbling with his suitcase, he kissed his mother on a charred cheek. He shook his father's hand with a perfunctory grip. He climbed aboard as the train began to clunk and crash in preparation. Looking out through the compartment window, he saw again this couple who had conspired to bring him about. He saw them for the first or last time. They stood, slung against each other as though they'd toppled that way, hands clasping, shoulders pressed, waiting for erosion to complete their collapse. As he watched, a small blizzard of leaves blew across them, so that they became fragmented and faded – as if already only remembered.

Fiction by
DAMON GALGUT
available from Atlantic Books include

Small Circle of Beings
'A novelist of great and growing power.' Rian Malan

The Beautiful Screaming of Pigs
'Engaging and enduring... devastating in the lucidity
and austere assurance of its prose.' *TLS*

The Quarry
'A writer of immense clarity and control.'
Patrick Ness, *Guardian*

The Good Doctor
'A lovely, lethal, disturbing novel.'
Christopher Hope, *Guardian*

The Impostor
'Outstanding... a major writer worthy to be referred to as a
kindred spirit of the great Coetzee.' *Irish Times*

In a Strange Room
'Acute, beautiful, unsettling. I have rarely felt so moved
whilst reading.' Sarah Hall, *The Times*

Arctic Summer
'A masterly piece of fiction. Delicate and detailed.' *Daily Mail*

Also available as E-books
www.atlantic-books.co.uk